MOUNTAIN GRUMP

BOSSY SINGLE DAD
BOOK 2

WILLOW FOX

ALLISON WEST

SLOWBURN
PUBLISHING

ONE

Logan

"I SWEAR if I hear one more complaint from the tourists, I'm going to walk out of this resort and never come back," I grumble.

"Is owning a ski resort really that bad?" Levi asks over the phone.

We've been friends since we served together in the army. However, we don't see each other very often. And it's not about the money. Levi inherited his father's business, a global hotel chain.

I made some early investments in a few tech companies that I'd never heard of and thought I'd be lucky if I had enough for retirement in forty years. Instead, I ended up a billionaire.

I guess I got lucky.

My luck seems to have run out, though.

I bought a ski resort in Montana. The place needed renovations and what I thought would be the hard part is over. Except that was a breeze. The contractors blew through the original estimate like water and found every expense in the book to tack on.

I'd never hire them again, but the place is mostly done. Four times over budget. And I've got to make up the money somehow. Adding a few dollars per ticket for an entrance fee helps, but it'll take years to recoup my investment.

"Oh, the logistics are great. The resort itself is gorgeous. It's like your house times three."

Levi chuckles. "Are we seriously measuring how big our houses are and comparing?"

I let the innuendo slide. I hadn't meant what he's suggesting.

"How's Julianna?" Levi asks.

Julianna is fifteen and ready for college. She wants to go away to school, move out of the country if she can, and be as far from her old man as possible.

I'm not keen on that arrangement, and just because I have the money doesn't mean I'm flushing it down the toilet for an education in drinking.

If she gets into a top-notch school, I'll handle the tuition, but she's not going to Oxford on her current GPA. And I'm not letting her fly to England or Paris to get the same degree she could get here just because she wants to travel the world.

She can take a gap year.

But I'm not funding it.

I didn't come from money, and I don't want her to think it isn't hard-earned, even if I got lucky.

"She's on holiday break," I say, and scratch the back of my neck. "New school has her a bit overwhelmed, I think, too. You should come out with Amelia. Julianna would love to see her."

"Do you think you have room for us at your place?" Levi asks, poking fun at me.

"I think we can spare a room. I mean, I could just charge you double, since I'm sure you'll be the biggest pain in the ass in the entire lodge."

"I can't be any worse than the grandmothers who try to take their grandkids skiing," Levi says.

He's not wrong.

Julianna is out of breath, jogging toward me and coming into my office. "I have to go." I hang up before I can give a proper send-off to Levi. He'll understand.

"What's wrong?" I ask, glancing her up and down. Why the hell is she running around?

"The floor out there is crazy crowded, and you're in here, hiding," Julianna groans. "I can't believe you're making me work floor duty."

"I'm not making you mop the floors." My gosh, the kid knows how to lay it on thick.

"You deal with the customers, Dad. See what it's like behind the actual desk, not in your office."

She's snarky today. She bit off more than she can chew.

"Fine." I slide my chair back, step around my desk, and out of the office. I head down the corridor and to the lobby, where half a dozen guests are waiting to be checked in at the ski rental stand.

I groan and redirect the guests to the correct side of the building. We have a hotel on the east side, and on the west side is the ski resort, which is open to the public. It isn't that difficult to understand. Signs and maps are all over the building, but it's newly laid out, and some people don't like change.

I check with Wyatt, my brother, to make sure the ski equipment is being handled properly. When guests rent their skis, they have to hand over their driver's license, and we hold on to it until the items are returned.

Everything looks above board, but he's drowning trying to help guests fast enough as the line keeps growing for rental equipment.

And they don't pay inside where they rent the skis. We have a separate booth for payment when guests first enter. It's supposed to be set up for ease, but I'm not sure it's the best method. We're still working out the kinks.

Julianna scurries behind the counter to help hand out ski boots. We're packed for a Tuesday, but it's also winter break for the kids in Breckenridge and surrounding towns. Barely a week until Christmas. Where did the year go?

I cover the equipment desk for a couple of hours. When it finally slows down, I head across the hallway to grab a bottle of water from my fridge.

"I can't believe these prices!" a woman's voice carries from within our shop.

I should just leave it alone and ignore the woman's complaints. Did she think she'd go on vacation and not spend a cent?

But I run the place and need to take customer complaints and issues seriously. Even Julianna reminded me that if I don't listen to what other people want, I can't help with fixing things. The kid is too smart for her own good.

"May I help you?" I answer gruffly.

There are two store attendants on duty. One is nestled behind the register, the other is folding T-shirts, and his eyes widen, noticing me. I guess staff doesn't necessarily expect the owner to be hands-on, but I'm not going to sit in my office all day.

My daughter would never let me if I wanted to.

"Three hundred dollars for a jacket is absurd. Can you believe that?" the brunette scoffs. "It's highway robbery. I didn't come here to get taken advantage of." She shoves the ski parka back onto the rack.

"It's winter, and you're at a ski resort. What did you expect?" I snap.

"I could buy this same coat at a department store for half the cost."

"Well, then maybe you should go and do that. You'll also want to embroider *Breckenridge* onto the front," I say, pointing at the customization that a lot of tourists enjoy.

"I could do that myself for half the cost," she huffs. "And the tickets for the ski lift, my gosh, families will need a second mortgage if they want to rent the equipment too. I hear there's a new owner. It's like he wants to shake your pockets and steal all your lunch money while you're on the lift."

Harsh.

"No one's forcing you to take the ski lift or go on the slopes. There's plenty to do in town if you're here for a nice, relaxing holiday."

Why am I still conversing with this woman? She's trouble. I can downright feel the intensity and heat of her fiery blue gaze.

"Well, they may not be forced, but this is a ski resort, and the classes, don't get me started on the costs of learning to ski. The lessons are exorbitant."

"Not everyone needs a class. There are bunny hills for those just getting started."

"You come here a lot?" Blue eyes asks, glancing me up and down.

I give a curt nod. "You could say that."

"Season ticket holder, huh?" she guesses.

She's wrong, but I don't correct her.

"Did you like the place better before the new jackass owner took over and changed everything? I hear he's a real stickler to the employees. Doesn't let them have time off and makes them work long hours. Have you noticed any of that?"

"I can't say that I have," I seethe.

"Oh, good," the woman says, smiling at me. She's all sunshine, and I'm the storm about to rain on her good day. She glances me up and down again. "The service here is lacking if you ask me. I had to wait twenty minutes to get into the right line for check-in."

"Did you follow the yellow arrows on the floor?" I growl as my hands bunch into fists at my sides.

"What arrows?" She shrugs, not having noticed the bright yellow and orange writing on the floor that pointed in the direction of *guest check-in*.

"Some people can't read," I mutter.

How is that my fault? If you can't follow instructions and it takes you twice as long, that's on you.

She glances at the next rack, with long-sleeved base layer tops for women. "Seventy dollars?" She scoffs at the price tag. "It's worth thirty."

"Have you ever been to a ski *resort*?" I ask, emphasizing the part where this is a vacation destination for folks who like snow. People fly in from all over the world. At least, that's the hope.

"What did you expect for clothes at a place like this to cost you?" I bite, my tone sharper than I intend.

"Oh, I don't know. I never really do ski resorts. It's usually beach vacations and whatnot. I'm an influencer."

"An influencer? Who the hell are you influencing, teens, on that clock app?" I huff, annoyed. This woman is wasting my time.

She purses her lips. "What I do is more like vlogging. But I've been known to dabble."

"Of course you have," I mutter. What the hell is vlogging? I need to get back to work. I turn and head out of the store without so much as a goodbye or farewell.

"Dad!" Julianna calls for me, coming out from behind the counter.

I pause and turn around, waiting for my daughter to catch up. Dare I even ask what it is?

"Is that Cali Sinclair?" Julianna asks, her eyes wide.

"I don't know. Is she a celebrity or something?" I've never heard of the woman Julianna is asking me about.

"Cali Sinclair is a vacation blogger. She reviews the next top destination spot. It's like whatever she posts always goes viral. The places are sold out for months if it's a good review. If it's bad, she destroys you."

I don't believe she has that kind of power. She's a woman with a phone, maybe a computer.

"I'm going to find out, Dad. We need the best publicity we can get!" Julianna squeals and hurries across the hallway. I grab her arm to stop her, but she slips by and rushes toward the woman.

I can't watch. I head back to my office. I have more important matters to attend to that need my intention, and trying to impress some girl who likes to make dancing videos isn't going to help me turn a profit.

———

I never did grab that bottle of water.

My office is chilly; the vents are open, and the heat is cranked up. The rest of the lodge is plenty warm, which means the heat isn't filtering in properly to the office.

Something I'll deal with another day.

I stalk out of the room, heading toward the lounge for a coffee.

The brunette from earlier is seated near the coffee machine, her leg up with a bag of ice melting faster than a popsicle.

She must have injured herself while out on the slopes.

"Hey, I didn't catch your name," the woman says as I stalk past her.

I should have grabbed a coffee from the pot in the back room, where I wouldn't have to interact with guests. My mistake.

But the coffee in the lounge is a million times better. I punch in the code for the coffee I want and then the admin code so I don't have to pay five dollars for a basic cup of coffee. It lets me bypass putting cash into the machine.

I grab the piping-hot cup and glance at the brunette. "I didn't give it," I say. She's cute, but there's only so much room for one grump in this lodge. I'd sooner throw myself down the black diamond slopes than spend five more minutes listening to her rant.

"Can you get me a coffee?" she asks, and holds up a five-dollar bill.

"Sure." I snatch the money and pocket it while punching in the code, getting her the same drink as I have. "Do you want cream and sugar?"

"Yes, please." She brightens up as I hand her the cup.

"Thank you," she says, taking a sip.

"First time on the slopes?" I ask, glancing at her ankle.

"Oh, this? No, that was from my heels."

"Seriously? Who the hell wears heels to a ski resort?" I glance her over, and while she's still in her navy leggings and pink shirt, she has a pair of boots with heels beside the chair.

Who the hell invented boots that can't be worn in winter?

"I didn't come here to go skiing," she says.

I perch myself, leaning forward over one of the chairs, giving her my undivided attention. I'm not sure why. I should get back to my office and leave this crazy chick alone. She's not doing me any favors, but making me question my sanity.

"You came here with these fashion boots to use the clock app and try to go viral?"

"Something like that. I'm Cali," she says, holding out her hand to introduce herself.

"Logan," I mutter, and shake her hand before taking another swig of coffee. I need an espresso, something stronger, to keep me focused this afternoon.

"I take it you don't like to ski?"

"Why would you say that?" I ask. Finishing the empty cup of coffee, I toss the cup into the nearby garbage and punch the digits into the machine. This time, I have it prepare me a double espresso.

Cali watches with fascination. "You're inside on a bitter day when it's frigid and snowy. Perfect ski weather. Also the kind of weather I despise."

"Why come here?"

"I told you, for work. I'm an influencer."

"Right." I can't imagine who she's influencing. Who would listen to her? "Your job makes zero sense. Aren't you supposed to try something out before judging it?"

"I'm not reviewing the ski slopes."

"But that's why people come to Blue Sky Resort. They don't come to the lodge because of the coffee or the jackets at the shop down the hall. They come for the experience of skiing or snowboarding on the slopes."

"Agree to disagree," Cali says.

I can't take much more of this woman. My espresso is ready, and I grab it from the machine. I should head back to my office. "On second thought," I say, sizing her up. "With your ankle injury as a result of your heels, you're a liability. Stay away from the slopes."

Her eyes narrow, and her nose twitches. "Why do you care? Do you work here? Wait, are you Logan Henderson?"

I bring my espresso to my lips and turn, heading out of the lounge before she can assault me with any more questions.

"Dad!" Julianna chases me down the hallway. I slow down to let her catch up while I sip the last of my drink. "Oh my gosh, Cali is so awesome!"

I groan, wishing that menacing woman had never showed up at the lodge in the first place. Who comes to a ski resort and doesn't plan on skiing?

"Not now, Jules," I snap at her.

Julianna stops walking and folds her arms across her chest. "Dad, do you have to steal the joy out of everything?"

Her words cut me deep. I didn't mean to do anything offensive. Why is she barking at me? "What is it?"

"I showed Cali the videos that I've done, and she's impressed. She invited me to intern with her this summer," Julianna squeals. I've never seen her so happy. Well, not since her mother and I divorced.

She's jumping up and down, eyes radiant as the sun. "You have to let me go, Dad. Please."

"I don't have to do anything. Where is it?"

"California."

"Of course it is," I mutter. "Cali is from California. Is that even her real name?"

"I don't know." Julianna shrugs.

"What do you even know about this woman?" I ask, steering Julianna into my office. I shut the door, not wanting anyone to overhear our private discussion.

"What's there to know? She offered to teach me everything related to vlogging and influencing. It's so cool, Dad. You have to say yes. Please. I want to be an influencer. I can make a lot of money at it, and you won't have to support me."

I rub my eyes, trying not to roll them back into my head. "Influencing isn't a job. It's a hobby."

"You don't know that," she argues. "You should talk to Cali."

"I already have," I seethe, and there's no way I want my fifteen-year-old hanging out with her over summer break next year. Not only do I not trust the woman because she's a stranger, but I also don't want Julianna getting any crazy ideas that she can be a vlogger.

"Wait, you did? She asked you about me interning for her?"

"No," I growl, and gesture for Julianna to sit across from me at the empty seat by my desk. I lean back on the desk, but I can't sit for this conversation.

"Oh." Julianna's face falls. "I knew I should have waited to ask until you were in a good mood, but that happens like never."

The kid is mouthy today. Probably part of her being a teenager and her hormones or something. It hasn't been easy, just the two of us. Her mom didn't even ask for joint custody when we divorced. She gave me Julianna but wanted the house in Greece. Like our kid is worthy of that kind of shitty trade?

Jess still irks me, the mere thought of her. I don't want another Jess hanging around Julianna, and I worry Cali will be no better, with her head in the clouds, convincing my innocent kid that she can be the next great influencer and go viral.

"We can talk about you accepting an internship later, but it's not going to be for some random girl who shows up at our lodge," I say. "We don't fraternize with the guests."

"What does that even mean, Dad? I'm not sleeping with her."

I choke back a laugh. Thank heaven, because the woman is too old to be bedding my daughter. "Is that what this is about, a crush?" I ask.

Julianna hasn't been secretive about her girl crushes. She's had more of those than boy crushes over the years. I think she's still figuring out her sexuality, and it's not something I want to discuss with a fifteen-year-old. She can date whomever she wants, as long as I meet them and approve.

And I don't approve of Cali. She's closer to my age. Well, in between. I'm forty-three. She's what, maybe twenty-five? I'll look her up later when my daughter isn't glaring at me.

"Cali isn't a crush. I mean, I'd die if she'd look at me that way, but she's fourteen years older than I am, Dad. Like, eww."

I laugh and do the mental calculation. That makes Cali twenty-nine. Fifteen years younger than I am.

Why do I care?

It's not like I'm interested in dating her.

Absolutely not. I've sworn off women since Jess did a number on my heart, tap dancing, stomping, and then flushing what was left of it down the toilet.

If it weren't for Julianna, I'd probably hate all women. But I love my kid, even if she doesn't know what's in her best interest. That's what I'm here for, to remind her and keep her on the straight and narrow.

"Seriously though, Dad, Cali invited us to dinner tonight."

"What?" I growl. I've heard enough. "Get back to work."

"Come on. You can't say no. I already told her I'd join her, and she wants to meet you."

My hands bunch into fists at my side. My biceps twitch with rage. "We've already met." I don't need to spend a meal with the woman to know I don't want my daughter around her. "And you shouldn't be making decisions without me."

"It's just dinner, and it's at the place you own. It's not like I'm going to her house in the middle of nowhere." Her voice rises, but she's not screaming at me. Julianna is irritated, her cheeks are red, and her dark hair in a bun is messy and starting to untangle and fall around her face.

She's right. I'm not entirely being fair. If she wants to have dinner with someone while at the lodge, I won't stop her. Hell, I'd be a hypocrite if I did. I've been telling her to make friends and get out there. I just wasn't expecting it to be with a grown-ass adult.

"You can have dinner with her. I've got work to do." I push myself off the desk and climb around to the leather chair, putting my ass down to make a point. I'll skip dinner if I must, but more than likely, I'll just grab something and bring it back to my office.

"Fine, be a grump," Julianna says, and storms out of my office.

"Teenagers," I mutter.

"Grumpy dads!" Julianna shouts back.

TWO

Cali

THE TEEN GIRL I met this afternoon was sweet and cute. Reminds me a bit of myself when I was her age.

I stay seated on the plush chair in the lounge. There aren't too many that are that comfy, and since my leg is elevated on an ottoman, I don't want to chance someone stealing my seat if I get up.

Which doesn't help, because I have to go pee really bad.

Coffee didn't help that, either.

But I'll just wait until dinner and deal with it then.

Which is sometime soon. My watch broke when I twisted my ankle, which was more like falling onto the floor than I'd like to admit.

I tripped, broke a heel, and bruised my knee while turning my ankle. I have the best luck in heels.

"Cali!" Jules waves as she notices me and jogs over. "I thought we were meeting by the restaurant?"

"Oh, we were supposed to. I'm sorry, my watch broke earlier, and my phone is out of juice." I show her the dead screen.

"Yikes. My dad would be so mad if I let my phone die. Then he couldn't reach me." She gives me a wicked grin before eyeing my ankle. "Do you need help to the restaurant?"

"I think I can manage," I say, and wince when I stand and put pressure on my ankle.

It's painful, and I bite down on my bottom lip to stifle the agony. I've done worse. I'm a klutz. It happens.

Cali offers me her shoulder. "You can lean on me," she says.

She's a good kid.

"Are we meeting your dad for dinner?" I ask. "Maybe he can help get us to the restaurant." I'm only half-joking. It's across the other side of the lodge, but at least it's not a hike on an incline.

"No, he can't come. He's busy," Jules says.

"Oh, okay. Is he still on the slopes?" I'm surprised he's not joining his daughter while on vacation.

"No, he's got work."

"Oh." I nod. He's probably got to deal with stuff back at the office in his hotel room. "Maybe he'll come down when he's done and join us."

"Maybe." She forces a smile, and I can't imagine how anyone could disappoint this kid.

Jules helps me through the giant room in the lodge to the hallway. We still have quite a walk to go, and I'm grimacing but holding back any moans. I don't want to worry her or scare the kid into calling for help. I'm sure I'll walk it off and be fine in the morning.

I try not to put too much weight on Jules' shoulders as I hobble toward the restaurant. "How long are you vacationing at Blue Sky?" I ask.

"Vacationing?" She starts laughing hysterically. "Cali, I live here."

"Oh, wow. That's neat. I didn't realize there were condos at the resort."

"Well, there's one for the owners," Jules says.

I cough and clear my throat. "Wait." I stop walking. I can't keep up with the conversation and physically move as I try to wrap my brain around what she's saying. "Your father is Logan Henderson?"

"That's right." She nods and gestures for the hallway. "If we don't keep walking, we won't make it by morning."

"Very funny," I say, and nudge her. We cross the main hall, and I swear it gets bigger the longer it takes to walk across, but we still have to go through the long, winding hallway between the ski resort and lodge for the restaurant. "Maybe you should grab us a table."

"I'm not sure you're going to make it," Jules says, and pulls out her phone.

"Who are you calling? I'll be fine." I don't want her calling 911 or anything over a sprained ankle. It's no big deal. Isn't the first time that I've been a klutz.

"Dad," Jules says, "I need your help. Cali got hurt."

A minute later, she hangs up the call, and his heavy footsteps follow him into the hallway.

"Jules, are you okay?"

"I'm fine. It's Cali," she says, gesturing at me. "I tried helping her to the restaurant, but we need crutches or a wheelchair. Is there something around that we can use?"

Logan glances me up and down. "Ankle bothering you?"

"Well, it's certainly not being very nice," I quip.

He doesn't look amused. "Here, I've got you," he says, and swoops me up, carrying me in his arms.

"Mr. Henderson, this isn't necessary," I say, trying not to laugh. Pressed against his chest, he smells fantastic, like pine and oak. His biceps are huge, and his chest is rock solid, all abs. I don't have to see it to feel it against me.

"Wrap your arms around my neck," he instructs as he carries me with ease down the hallway, and in less than a minute, we're at the restaurant. We bypass the long line of guests waiting for a table.

A few people grumble their dissatisfaction as he carries me to the back of the restaurant. There's a booth that typically seats four, with a placard that says *Reserved* on it. I can only assume it's for his daughter and him.

He gently places me down in the booth, and I untangle my arms from around his neck. "Um, thank you," I say, feeling flustered. My stomach is full of butterflies, and I'm not sure why. Is it his dark, brooding eyes or the way he stares at me, straight into my soul?

"Don't mention it," he answers, and I feel like he means it. He never wants me to speak of it again.

"I'm glad you'll be joining us," I say.

"Keep your leg elevated in the booth. I'll go back to the kitchen and fetch you fresh ice."

"That's my dad," Jules says, smiling awkwardly as she points at him. "Please don't hate him. He's the biggest grump, but I promise I'm nothing like him. If I intern for you, I won't be a constant grouch."

"I would hope not." I chuckle. "I'm sure your dad isn't that bad." I force a smile. When I met him earlier, he seemed quite cold and distant, but I also hadn't realized with whom I was speaking.

I groan and cover my face with my hands. "Oh my gosh, Jules. I totally bitched about this place to your father. The owner!"

How the hell am I going to get an interview with him after that debacle? I'm lucky he hasn't kicked me out and banned me from ever returning.

Well, there's still time for me to muck up the assignment. I swear Bridget sent me out here to get even with me. She told me I needed a change of scenery, and my vlogging was becoming too routine for their site.

That's code for boring.

Logan returns, carrying a sealed bag of ice wrapped in paper towels. "Your leg should be elevated higher," he scolds.

"I can't get it any higher, and it's already on the bench."

He rests the cold pack of ice over my ankle, and I grimace from the chill and initial contact. That other bag had turned to warm water a couple of hours ago.

"Enjoy your dinner," Logan says.

"Dad, wait! You're already here."

His jaw is firm and tight.

"Please," I say, gesturing for him to sit across from me and next to his daughter, since my leg is taking up the rest of the booth.

He sighs and relents, joining us at the table. "I have a lot of work to do, young lady," he says, glaring at Jules.

She smiles and sits up, shoulders back like she's proud of her accomplishment.

I open my mouth but then shut it. I need to be careful how I tread. When I was inviting Jules to intern, I didn't realize her father was the resort's owner.

From what I know about Logan Henderson, he's a billionaire. It's considerably new money, and he's single. Although the last one I'm guessing, based on him not wearing a wedding band.

I can't assume anything. He could be getting it resized.

Jules hasn't mentioned her mother, and now isn't the time to ask.

"I'm sorry about earlier," I say, staring at Logan, hoping we can move past the awkwardness.

A waitress comes over, bringing three water glasses along with silverware and menus.

Logan reaches for his glass and takes a sip, his eyes never leaving mine. "Go on," he says.

I wasn't planning on elaborating, but if he wants a huge apology, I'll suck it up and give it to him to stroke his ego. Although that's not the only thing I'd like to stroke.

I bite my bottom lip, trying to tame the wayward thoughts.

He has a teenage daughter. For all I know, he could be happily married. Although his wife certainly didn't come down for dinner.

Interesting.

Maybe he *is* single.

Logan raises an eyebrow when I don't say anything. "You were saying," he urges me to continue my apology.

Bastard.

I almost don't want to continue apologizing, because if he needs his ego stroked, then what kind of a man is he?

"I was saying that I'm sorry for over-speaking earlier. Sometimes I let my mouth run in front of my head."

Jules chuckles. "I like her, Dad."

"Yeah, you would," he mutters.

I exhale a hearty sigh. I didn't invite him to dinner to fight with him. Technically, I didn't ask *him* to dinner. I invited Jules' father. I just didn't realize they were the same person.

Yikes. Awkward. I'd be better off throwing myself down the ski slopes without equipment. Let my ankle take one for the team. Well, maybe my entire body.

"Anyways," I say, trying to change the subject, "your daughter was telling me she's interested in what I do for a living."

Logan sips his water again, and as he puts it down on the table, his eyes tighten. "I wouldn't constitute what you do as a career choice. Tell my daughter that it's not a way to make a living, that you live paycheck to paycheck, and there are better opportunities out there."

I'm taken aback by his bluntness. "You look down on what I do," I say.

"As I said, you can't make a living at it."

"I live comfortably," I say. "It wasn't easy, and freelancing didn't add up to much in my case, but if you choose to work for the right agency or company, you can make six figures."

"Don't fill Julianna's head with wild ideas," Logan says. "There's no way you're making six figures a year."

"Do you want to see my bank statements?" I retort. I don't intend to show him, even if he does say yes.

His expression is grim, and his nostrils flare. "That isn't necessary."

"You don't like me, Mr. Henderson."

"What makes you think that? Was it you insulting the store, our remodeling, or throwing yourself on the floor for attention?"

I scoff at his suggestion. "I may have insinuated that the prices for your store are above average and distinguishing between the ski lodge and resort was confusing. But I did not throw myself on the floor for anyone's attention, least of all yours."

Logan stands.

"Dad, where are you going?" Jules asks as her voice hitches.

"Where I should have gone after getting your friend ice," he sneers at me.

I open my mouth but quickly shut it. I'm not getting my interview tonight. That's a given. The man is moody as hell and irritating. It doesn't help that he's easy on the eye, with dark hair and a beard. I swear his beard is longer than the hair he keeps trimmed on his head.

He's hot, but he's not my type.

Arrogant.

Brash.

A billionaire.

Yeah, I don't chase men, least of all ones who despise me. And Mountain Grump hates my guts. He could totally be a mountain man, all reclusive and avoiding civilization. It would be more fitting than the man running a ski resort.

How the hell did he wind up here, owning Blue Sky Resort?

Maybe the story isn't about the resort but the man behind it. Would that help put me over the edge for the vlog?

I let Mountain Grump charge away, and Jules looks distraught.

"I'm so sorry, Cali."

"It's fine," I say, and hold up my hands. The girl needs no explanation. "But do you think you could do me a favor?"

Her eyes light up. "Anything."

"I need to make some videos for the vlog. Can you help with that?" I ask. I'm unsure of the best places to film, and I'd love to get some behind-the-scenes shots. With Jules' help, I may have access to some areas I wouldn't ordinarily be able to go to.

"Of course, but we can't tell my dad."

I purse my lips and pretend to lock them.

We shouldn't be keeping secrets from her father. It's a bad start for gaining his trust and getting a one-on-one interview.

But I need Jules' help even more, since I can't put any weight on my ankle.

"That's fine. I don't think your dad likes me very much."

She chuckles. "He's like that with everyone, not just you."

I want to ask her about his status and whether he's single, but it doesn't feel appropriate. Why do I even need to know, other than aching curiosity? He's gorgeous, with his tattoos and gruffness. There's something raw and sexy about him that makes my knees weak.

That could be why I tripped over my own two feet. I was glancing over my shoulder. I thought I saw him in the hallway, but I was mistaken. It was someone else in blue jeans and a dark-gray T-shirt.

The man is absolutely sinful.

I shouldn't be having these thoughts about him.

He's arrogant.

Thickheaded.

A pain in the ass.

Even if he did carry me down the hallway and put me ever so gently down into the booth, just remembering it makes my cheeks warm, and my stomach fills with butterflies.

"Are you feeling all right, Cali? Your face is all red and flushed."

I grab my water glass, hoping to cool myself off. "I'm fine. It's just been a while since I've eaten anything." Or gotten laid. But I leave the last thought off.

THREE

Logan

I'M UP EARLY, before the sun.

"Dad." Julianna slips into my office in her pajamas. She's wearing oversized flannel pants and a dark-red top to go with the ensemble. Her eyes are heavy, and she's latched on to a mug of coffee.

I could use my caffeine fix this morning.

I glance up from my paperwork, going over the numbers for the third time. I have an accountant who helps and double-checks everything, but I prefer to keep in control of the numbers because I need to know how much is coming in and going out regularly.

"Yes?" I ask as she pulls me away from my work.

"Is it okay if I invite a friend from school over today?"

A huge smile grazes my face. "I would be delighted to meet one of your friends." Since moving here over the summer, Julianna hasn't made a lot of friends, or if she has, she hasn't seen them outside of class. But it's winter break, so I'm hoping she'll do more than just work for the resort for the next two weeks.

"Izzie's cool, and she says she can snowboard."

"One of her parents will need to sign a liability waiver," I say.

"I know, Dad. You don't have to worry. Izzie is really good on the slopes."

"Even so, she still needs a parent or guardian's permission and the form filled out."

Julianna rolls her eyes and groans. "Fine. I'll make sure she has it done."

"And I'd like to meet her parents."

"Oh my gosh! Why do you have to be so cringe?"

"Cringe?" I ask, shaking my head. I put my pen down and rest my hands on my desk. When did my teenage daughter become such a handful?

"Like, you know, embarrassing?"

I stand and step around the desk. "All parents are cringe when you're fifteen." I wrap my arms around my daughter in a hug, and she groans like it's torture.

"Not all. Izzie's parents are cool. Her dad works for this investigation firm. They're like private investigators, hostage negotiators. They save people's lives."

I loosen my grip around Julianna. "What's her dad's name?"

"I don't know. They both work for the company."

"Well, when her mom or dad drops her off at the resort, I'd like to meet them."

"Fine." She rolls her eyes at me and heads out of my office.

The smell of Julianna's coffee permeates the small space, even without her in it. I grab my empty mug and head down to the lounge.

Cali is seated across from the coffee machine, book in hand. Her dark hair frames her features, and I try to sneak by without having to say hello.

"Thanks again for helping me last night," she says.

I glance over my shoulder as she puts her book down, a bright, sunny smile on her face.

"It was nothing." I punch the code into the coffee machine and wait for it to brew a latte.

"Carrying me across the hallway wasn't nothing," she says, insisting that I acknowledge her appreciation.

"How's your ankle this morning?" I ask. She's got her foot up on the ottoman, but she's not icing it.

"Better." She lifts her pants leg to reveal an elastic bandage wrap. "I tend to be clumsy." Her smile lights up the room, and all I want to do is sink back into the darkness of my office.

Why am I so glum? Moving was supposed to help me refocus and move past Jess, the woman who ripped out my heart when I walked in on her with another man in my bed.

I force a smile. "You should pick up a pair of flats in the shop."

"No, thanks. I don't need to spend on a pair of overpriced and uncomfortable shoes in your store."

"They're actually quite comfortable. Julianna helped pick out the women's slippers and boots that we sell."

"Well, then I might have to glance at them if your daughter is the one responsible for your inventory."

She slides her foot off the ottoman and gestures for me to have a seat.

Does she think I enjoy conversing with her? I grab my latte that's finished and consider dumping it for black coffee. There's only so much sweetness that I can handle in one morning, and Cali wins that award.

"Sit." Cali gestures for me to join her.

"I have work," I say, and glance at my watch.

"You'll always have work. Make time for your guests."

Standing across from her, I exhale a heavy breath and sip my drink. "You should elevate your ankle. I'm not sitting."

"Fine," she says with an exasperated huff, and rests her ankle back on the ottoman. "Are you always this difficult?"

"Are you always this demanding?" I quip.

A wide grin captures her face. "Yes, most definitely. I realize we haven't exactly gotten off on the right foot." She grimaces at her words. "Can we start over?"

"It's not any big deal," I say.

"It is to me. Your daughter is bright and has some great ideas. She was showing me her videos on her phone, and I'm serious about wanting her to intern for me."

"And I'm serious about not letting her waste her talent on being an influencer. I'm happy it worked out for you, but my daughter needs more structure. She can't be chasing butterflies and marketing the next big craze to young minds."

"Is that what you think I do?" Cali asks. Her brow pinches, and I'm sure I've insulted her, albeit unintentionally. She can't help what she does for a living.

"I've worked with influencers before. They all tend to be young and bright-minded but think their follower count is tied to their self-worth. I don't want that for my daughter."

"Let me interview you, and then you can make a sound judgment on my job."

"You're not getting an interview," I say, finishing the rest of my drink in one swig. "You have a better chance of shooting a video of a bear riding a snowboard downslope than me talking to you on camera."

She quirks a grin.

She thinks I'm funny.

"I'll get that interview, Mr. Henderson."

I don't bother to correct her and tell her that she won't, over my dead body. I don't do the media. I don't speak to the press. I hate being the center of attention and in the spotlight.

"I have work to do," I say, and head out of the lounge without so much as a goodbye.

I swear I can feel the heat of her stare as she watches me walk out of the room.

"Dad!" Julianna barrels into me as she rounds the corner. "I've been looking for you. Izzie is here with her mom."

I follow Julianna across the hall and toward the main entrance. Izzie is a bit punk with her black leather jacket and denim skirt. She's got thick black eyeliner that accents her blue eyes.

"Hi, I'm Logan," I say, holding out my hand to introduce myself.

"Ariella," the woman says, "this is my daughter, Izzie."

"Stepdaughter," Izzie says with a smile. "Please don't tell us we look alike."

I wouldn't dream of it. The kid is punk gothic, and the woman has her hands full. I can relate. Do I need to worry that this phase might rub off on my daughter?

"Izzie mentioned that you needed me to sign a permission slip?"

I quirk a grin. "This isn't school, but I need a parent or guardian to sign a liability waiver. It's a requirement for all guests."

"That's fine. Lead the way."

I escort her toward our check-in desk, where guests typically have to pay for a day pass. I grab the forms behind the counter, handing them to Ariella. "Are both of you joining us today?"

"No, just me," Izzie says, and watches as her stepmom fills out the forms. "I've been doing this since I was a kid."

After Ariella leaves, I ensure the girls are comfortable going out onto the slopes alone. Izzie has spent plenty of hours at the resort snowboarding, long before I owned the place. It's a relief not to have to worry about them.

I remind both girls to stay together on the trails before heading to check on the rest of the staff.

Cali wanders into the shop, and I watch from across the hall, curious if she will have another fit regarding our prices.

I should wander back into my office and ignore the woman who has caused me nothing but a headache.

At least Julianna is distracted with her friend today and not yammering on about Cali and her social media presence. I might have to lock myself in my office and not return until that woman leaves the resort.

When she heads toward the register with a box in hand, I take that as a good sign that she's not being belligerent with my staff.

"Do you always stand out in the hallway staring at pretty women?" Wyatt asks.

I glare at my brother. "I don't know what you're talking about."

Is it that obvious?

"Liar," Wyatt says with a laugh. "Jules told me about your little kerfuffle with Cali Sinclair. Are you going to liquor her up and convince her to write a puff piece about this place?"

"That would be unethical," I grumble.

"But a whole lot of fun," Wyatt quips. "I haven't seen you that transfixed over a girl since—well, honestly, never."

I raise an eyebrow and turn to face him.

I don't say it, but he does.

"Jess wasn't the right girl for you. Yes, she gave you Julianna, but that's it. You deserve to be happy."

I huff at his remark. I don't deserve anything. "Can we not talk about Jess?" Her name on my tongue makes my stomach sour.

Wyatt grins like I just took the bait. "Are you going to ask *her* out? Because if you're still not interested in dating, I'd like to hook up with her."

I growl and grab his shirt, pushing him backward several strides, and shoving him against the wall. "You're an asshole," I sneer.

"For liking a girl?" Wyatt asks.

"For suggesting a hookup. You don't even know her. She could be married."

"Jules tells me that she isn't."

That caught my attention. Why the hell does my daughter know the status of Cali's love life? "Even so, my place of business isn't a brothel. Keep your dick in your pants."

"Wow, just because you're not getting laid doesn't mean you need to take it out on the rest of us." Wyatt smirks and leans in closer. "If you wanted her for yourself, all you had to do was say as much. I've never seen you get jealous before, and it's not a pretty color on you."

"Get back to work," I snap, and step away from him.

Cali's soft footsteps trail closer as I turn around and see her coming toward me. "Are you always such a grump to all your employees?"

Wyatt glances back over his shoulder, catching part of the conversation, and I glare at him to keep moving.

"That employee is my brother," I mutter.

"Oh wow." Cali's eyes light up. "Is he part owner, too?"

If she goes after him for an interview and he accepts, I'll put him on toilet duty indefinitely.

"No. He works for me." I clear my throat and change the direction of the conversation away from her interest in Wyatt. "New shoes?"

She's donning fur-lined boots. They're flats, which should keep her from another injury. They're beige and fashionable. Nothing she can wear on the slopes, but I don't expect her to go out anytime soon after her recent ankle injury.

"I took your advice and bought myself a pair. I also used your discount."

"My what?"

"You know, the sleeping with the boss discount?" She smirks and winks at me before turning and heading down the hallway.

My jaw hangs open, and it takes a minute for me to catch up with her. I'm stunned by her remark. "We didn't sleep together. Did you hit your head?" I quip as I catch up to her.

"No, but I got a nice discount." Cali's smile is bright. "And your employee behind the register felt super bad for me. Apparently, you're a grump to all your employees."

"That isn't true." Why is this woman tormenting me? Did Wyatt put her up to it? Maybe he hired her to show up at the resort to make my life hell. I wouldn't put it past him, trying to get me laid and to move on.

"Don't believe it? Go ask him," she says. Cali is all smiles, and somehow, my grumpy disposition does nothing to affect her. Like she's immune to me. It's probably for the best. I'd ruin her if given a chance.

"I don't need to ask him anything. If you keep the shenanigans up, I will have to ask you to leave the resort."

"You can't kick me out. If you do, I'll make sure to create the most scathing review for your resort. It'll destroy you."

The woman is threatening me. I'm appalled that she thinks she has the power to take me down. "Good luck trying to get anyone to read your little blog."

"You really don't know who I am," Cali says.

"Am I supposed to?" I ask. Julianna mentioned it yesterday, but I can't remember or care.

She smiles, tight-lipped, but doesn't say anything further. "It doesn't matter." She wanders down the hall, and it's impossible not to stare at her perfect ass as she sways her hips.

I swear she's doing it to steal my attention, and it's working. I need to stay away from her. She's a distraction with the kind of body that would fit perfectly with mine, pinning her under me, showing her who is in charge.

I'll bet she moans loudly when she comes, sweat coating every inch of her naked skin, head tilted back, eyes closed.

I can't let her affect me and get inside my head. Sleeping with her isn't appropriate. She's a guest, and I run the resort. That's the last type of review I need showing up anywhere: *Handsome Billionaire Bachelor gives private tours at the Blue Sky Resort. Expect your panties to be twisted in a knot as he ties you up and rails you off the slopes.*

Cali breezes past the equipment rental desk that Wyatt is managing. He smiles at her, and I want to growl at him for even paying attention to her.

She's mine.

FOUR

Cali

I DIDN'T ACTUALLY TELL the kid at the checkout counter that I'm sleeping with Logan, but I did ask if there's a friends and family discount.

For the record, there wasn't.

The shoes blow out my budget until my next paycheck, but this time it's something I need to splurge on. I can't risk another ankle injury, and I have a tendency to roll my ankles in heels.

Why the hell did I think it was wise to wear heels to a ski resort?

My phone buzzes as I head back to my room to unload my heels. I glance at the caller. It's Bridget, my boss.

She's probably calling to check up on the status of my interview. I haven't posted anything online since arriving, which is not good. She likes our accounts to be active, and since we typically post multiple times per day, my ignoring social media doesn't do us any favors.

"Hello," I answer, biting down on my bottom lip.

"Cali, how is it going? I haven't seen any online activity from you."

She gets right to the point. I rub my eyes. I'd rather lie down and nap than go in front of the camera right now and make a video. And Logan isn't going to let me film him. At least not willingly.

And his daughter is underage. While I'd love to have her help me, I can't put her on camera without his permission. We don't want to get sued.

"I've been trying to make contact with the owner."

"Logan Henderson?" Bridget asks. "Is he that hard to find?"

"Oh, he's constantly underfoot," I say a little too loudly.

"What's that, Cali?"

I grimace and inhale a deep breath.

Exhale.

I try to regroup my thoughts before I end up fired. "Logan is great. He's just not interested in interviewing with us or anyone else."

"I don't care how you get the interview, but I didn't send you to the resort for a free vacation. Do your job."

I roll my eyes, grateful she can't see my expression. "I am doing what I can to get in with Mr. Henderson. At the moment, I'm working an angle."

"What kind of angle?" Bridget perks up at the sound of me working and gathering information.

"He has a daughter. She's fifteen and knows who I am."

"Interesting." I swear there's a smirk adorning her face. "Use it. Is he single?"

"I don't know." I didn't notice a wedding band, but that doesn't mean he's not attached. I keep my mouth shut about the shoe incident earlier at the store. And how I told Logan that I informed the clerk I should get the shoes for free because I was sleeping with the owner.

Not my finest moment.

I was trying to flirt with him. The man is gorgeous, with dark ink on his arms and a brooding personality. I can't help but imagine what it must be like to be dominated by him in the bedroom. He doesn't seem like the kind of man who would go slow or be gentle.

I'm not complaining. I'd love to find my way under him, arms wrapped around his neck, my legs wrapped around his hips, holding him like a vice.

I turn the heat down in my hotel room. It's stifling.

"Well, find out, and if he is, ask him out for drinks. You can put it on the company card. But I need that interview."

"He's not going to let me film him," I say.

"It's fine. He doesn't have to be on camera. I mean, it'd be better if you could catch a shot of him coming out of the hotel pool, dripping wet. I've seen his picture, Cali. The man is pure eye candy."

I bite down on my tongue to keep from speaking and telling her he's not just good-looking, he's also Grumplicious. But that doesn't help my situation. "Do you suggest I stalk the pool?" I'm only half-joking. I could lie around in my swimsuit and read all afternoon, waiting for a glimpse of Logan.

"Do what you have to do."

Does the man swim in the hotel pool? Maybe he has a small pool upstairs in the penthouse suite where he lives.

I wonder if there's a way I can get up there and check it out? Julianna isn't likely to let me upstairs, and there's zero chance Logan will invite me to his suite. He'd sooner make me sleep outside in the snow.

I hang up with Bridget and put my swimsuit under my clothes. Just in case I get the opportunity to grab a rare picture of Logan Henderson in a swimsuit. Although, I'm kind of hoping he prefers to swim naked.

Although, that's not very likely in the hotel pool where guests are allowed to frequent.

I grab a towel and head down to check out the pool. A few noisy kids are swimming and splashing, soaking the lounge chairs. Most of them are fairly young, and their parents are in the room, not exactly supervising them.

Opting not to get soaked by kids, I head down the hallway and catch a glimpse of Logan in the fitness room. He's lifting weights, and I can't help but stand by the glass window and stare.

Seconds tick by, and I should keep moving. But I don't. He's handsome and sexy as hell. His face is red, the veins on his arms bulging with each flex.

That's not the only vein that I'm thinking about bulging. I shouldn't have such illicit thoughts about Logan. He's trouble. Positively off-limits. Sleeping with the owner of a resort is only going to sway my review. That would be unprofessional.

Unless I were writing a review about his sex appeal or how he performed in bed.

Logan Henderson is a giver. The man is a glorious grump with a 3-1 record of giving more orgasms than receiving.

Beneath his tough and stuffy exterior he puts on during the day, at night he's a wild lion in the sheets, searching for his lioness to pin down and devour.

He is a beast, and the longer I stare, the more guilty I look when he catches my gaze. I open my mouth, thinking my eyes must be wide like a doe, and I hurry down the hallway, pretending I wasn't just standing there ogling him.

Is there any chance he didn't notice?

With my towel in my hand, I head toward the elevators, and Jules waves at me excitedly. She's not alone. Beside her is a girl about her age, but with darker hair and a gothic punk look. The girl could seriously be in a band. She gives off a rockstar vibe.

"Cali!" Jules says. "This is my girlfriend, Izzie."

Izzie gives a sideways grin and wrinkles her nose. "Girlfriend?"

"What?" Jules asks, glancing back at her friend.

"I thought we weren't telling people. It was just between us," she hisses at her.

"Relax, she's cool, and she's not about to tell my dad. He hates her."

Izzie snickers and shoves her hands into her pockets. "Are you heading to the pool?" She nods toward the towel in my hand.

It's dry, along with the rest of me. Well, most of me. Staring at Logan didn't exactly keep me a saint.

I could use a dip in the water and cool off if there weren't a bunch of little kids in there. "I was going to but got distracted," I say as they lead me toward the pool and back through the hallway where I'd just been staring at Logan lifting weights.

He steps out of the fitness room, a towel slung over his neck, shirtless.

Is the man trying to give me a heart attack?

I trip over my feet, not paying attention to anything but the man with rock-hard abs. Is that the only thing that's rock hard?

With my feet coming out from under me, I jolt forward toward the floor. But Logan catches me, his arm around my waist, pulling me to his chest, not letting me hit the ground.

"Thanks," I say.

And if I wasn't embarrassed enough before, now I'm humiliated.

"I should go." I try to untangle myself from his arms, but he doesn't let go of me.

He glances down at my feet. The boots that I just bought are still secure. "Are the boots too big?" he asks, and his hands slide from my waist down to my feet, checking to see if there's too much room for my toes in the shoes.

"They fit fine," I say.

A few nearby guests gasp at the sight, and I inhale a sharp breath.

They pull out their cameras like they're trying to do us a favor by recording this event. But it's not what they think. He may be down on one knee, but he's not proposing.

He presses down with two fingers on the top of my soles, discovering that the boots indeed fit as they should.

Logan glances up, noticing the guests crowding around the hallway and watching us. "Nothing to see here." He gestures them all away, but it isn't until he stands that they decide to take his word for it and go about their merry way.

Jules and her friend Izzie exchange smiles and giggles before hurrying down the hallway, leaving the two of us behind.

"Well, that was awkward," I say, clutching the pristine white towel to my chest.

"People are so damn nosy," Logan mutters, and runs a hand through his short dark hair. "Are you okay?"

"I didn't fall," I point out, appreciating that he caught me. "I'll be fine."

"Maybe you should have a doctor examine you."

"Why? I'm fine."

"You've tripped twice, one time injuring yourself. The second could have been worse if I wasn't here."

Yeah, if he weren't here, I wouldn't have tripped. My attention was on the fact that he was shirtless and looking sexy as hell.

"We have a physician on-site. I can take you there, have him look you over to make sure you didn't hit your head."

"I'm fine, I promise. It's just my ankle, and it feels better. Maybe I twisted it back into place."

"That's not a thing," he says, his gaze never wavering.

"Well, it should be." I glance away, his stare too heated and intense for me. It's like he's staring right through my soul.

"Humor me. If the physician says everything is fine, I'll leave you alone."

"No, you'll buy me dinner, and this time, sit with me during our shared meal."

His eyes crinkle with mirth. "Are you asking me out, *Sunshine*?"

At least he's not calling me clumsy. "I wouldn't dream of it, *Grumpster*."

"That sounds like Dumpster," he huffs, clearly unamused. "That better not stick."

"Then don't be such a grump."

He growls and leans in. I swear he's about to kiss me. Maybe it's because I want him to kiss me. My lips tingle, and he sweeps me off my feet, his arm coming up under my legs as he carries me.

"Put me down!" I laugh, and while yesterday, his carrying me was romantic because my ankle hurt, today, I'm embarrassed by the attention he's giving me.

"Not until I've taken you to be checked out," he says.

"You've been checking me out," I say cheekily.

For a moment, I think he's going to drop me. I wrap my arms around his neck. It's the most romantic gesture a man's ever made, carrying me, and now he's done it twice.

There's silence between us and chatter in the halls as he carries me through the lodge and outside.

I grumble at the cold, wincing. Couldn't the physician be in the main building?

There's a medical building that isn't attached, but it will be one day. An overhang covers the top and plastic sheeting to keep the elements out but no heat.

I shiver, clinging closer and tighter to Logan.

"Sorry, we're almost there," he grumbles as we approach the door, and he backs up with his butt, hitting the handicap button to open the door automatically.

Logan carries me into the medical center with ease. It's a small waiting room out front, and he puts me down in one of the chairs.

"Mr. Henderson, how can I help you?" the receptionist asks.

"Cali took a tumble yesterday in the lodge. She twisted her ankle and then had another near miss walking in the hallway. I'd like the physician to look her over. Make sure there isn't something neurologically wrong with her."

"My head is fine. You're the one with the stick up your ass. Maybe you should have a doctor check to see how far it's been shoved up there."

I can't help the snarkiness, and Logan turns around and tilts his head, eyes wide. He looks shocked, or he's appalled by my remark.

Well, he has been a grumpy ass. What'd he expect? There's only so much of the man I can take. Unless we're talking sex, I can take one hundred percent of him inside of me.

My gaze moves over his body and down to his tight-fitting jeans.

The receptionist forces a smile. "You're already here. How about we have the physician look you over to make sure you're all right."

With two sets of eyes staring back at me, it's hard to say no. "You owe me dinner," I say, pointing at Logan.

"It would be an honor."

Somehow, I don't think he means it. He's putting on a show for the receptionist.

Why? Is he concerned that she might start a rumor about him sleeping with a guest? I'm sure there's better gossip around the lodge.

"Do you need a wheelchair to head back to one of the rooms?" the receptionist asks.

"No, I can walk," I say, and stand. I sway slightly, and it takes a few seconds for my feet to feel like they're back on land again.

The receptionist escorts me back to one of the rooms, and Logan hangs out by the front desk. She's the triage nurse, not just the receptionist.

She takes my blood pressure, pulse, and temperature before disappearing out of the room and leaving me alone.

My blood pressure is a little low, but that's not unusual for me. I've always had low blood pressure. As a teenager, I was told by a cardiologist to load up on salt and caffeine because I used to faint. I'm not sure that was the best advice, but it helped.

A few minutes later, a gentleman comes sauntering into the room.

"Hi, I'm Dr. Reynolds," he says. "I hear that you fell and hurt your ankle."

"My ankle is doing better. I tend to be clumsy, and the ogre out in the hallway insisted that I get checked out."

He raises a curious eyebrow. "Ogre?"

"Logan Henderson," I say.

"My boss." He grins and laughs. He's about Logan's age, but his hair is a little more salt and pepper, and he has less beard. Logan is all beard, thick, dark, and it accents his features. "How about we appease him for a few minutes and I examine your ankle, and if you can, I'd like to have you walk around on it."

"Sure," I say. He looks at my ankle, satisfied that there's no swelling and it doesn't hurt when he touches or tries to have me move it. He has me stand.

"Can you walk to the other side of the room and back?"

It's a small space, only a few steps, so I do as he instructs.

"Good," he says. "Now, I'd like you to walk a straight line. From heel to toe."

"Easy," I say, but when I try to do as he's asked, my gait staggers, and I sway.

His hands come out to make sure that I don't fall, but I catch myself.

"Have you had trouble with balance?" Doctor Reynolds asks.

"Not that I noticed."

"Stand with your feet together."

I do as he instructs, and the longer I stand, the more I sway to the left and catch myself, moving my legs apart to keep from falling over. "That doesn't seem normal," I say.

He doesn't answer my remark. And as much as I feel like Logan is brooding, this man's silence wins. My stomach flops.

"It's because I twisted my ankle. Right?"

"Sit for me," he says, and gestures to the chair.

He has me follow a penlight and quite a few other tricks. He doesn't indicate anything specific. "Did you go down the ski slopes?"

"No, I don't know how to ski. I've never been," I say.

"Do you have a primary care physician?"

"Back at home. I don't live around here."

"I recommend that you follow up with your primary care physician when you return home. It could be inner ear related, or they may want to give you a referral to a neurologist."

"What?" My voice squeaks.

"Are you having any issues with dizziness, vertigo, nausea, or hearing loss?"

"No," I say. "I'm just clumsy." At least, that's what I thought it was. I'm nervous. But maybe he's wrong. He's used to seeing broken bones and concussions all day. I'm not his usual type of patient.

After I finish with Dr. Reynolds, I head out into the hallway. Logan is waiting in one of the plastic chairs. He immediately stands when he sees me, his eyes wide. He wants to know what the doctor said.

"I'm fine." I brush him off and glance at the receptionist. "How much do I owe you?"

"It's already taken care of," she says, nodding toward Logan.

"It's on the house," Logan says, opening the door, letting me walk back as we head through the outside corridor.

I wrap my arms around myself, chilled from the news and the air temperature.

"Dinner?" he says, glancing at me, nudging me as we walk. His hand slips to my lower back, keeping me close.

I sigh, leaning into his touch. I don't want to tell him I'm terrified. The doctor's remarks weren't what I was expecting to hear. What made Logan insist on having me examined?

"I'm not hungry," I say. I lost my appetite when the doctor brought up possibly having to see a neurologist.

Logan opens the heavy glass door that connects to the lodge. A warm gust of air assaults me and is a welcoming relief from the frigid chill.

"I owe you dinner, and it's getting late," Logan says.

"What about your daughter?"

"She's with her friend. They won't miss me. We can sit down in the restaurant and have a bite, or I can make something upstairs."

"Upstairs?" I repeat. That catches my attention. "Is there another restaurant upstairs for VIP clients?" I hadn't seen anything online or in the brochure about an upstairs restaurant.

"I meant I'd cook for you."

"You know how to cook?" I can't hide the smile. I'm not sure why, but I don't imagine this man having labored in the kitchen for years. "You don't have a chef?"

"My chef is in the kitchen downstairs, at the restaurant," Logan says. "Just because I'm well off doesn't mean I can't do things for myself."

"Sorry," I say, quick to apologize. I didn't mean to insult him. "Is this kitchen part of your house or a private kitchen for your most elite guests?"

"It's in the penthouse suite."

He's inviting me up to his room. My feet sway slightly, and Logan's arm wraps around my hip.

"I swear if you fall again, I'm flying you to the nearest emergency room for a second opinion."

"Isn't that a little much?" While I should shrug off his touch, I don't dare admit I enjoy his arm wrapped around me.

"I'll decide what's necessary," he says.

He escorts me to the elevator and groans as another gentleman steps inside with us. "Wyatt," he mutters, apparently knowing the guy. Logan punches the button for the penthouse suite and shoves his key into the lock for access.

I offer a warm smile, and Logan wraps his arm possessively around my shoulders like he's claiming I'm with him.

Possessive much?

"Where are you two lovebirds off to?" Wyatt quips. There's a wry grin on his face.

I open my mouth to say that we're not anything, but Logan answers before I can.

"Cali, this is my younger brother, Wyatt."

"It's nice to meet you," I say, and offer my hand. I recall seeing him the other day now.

"Likewise. Are you sure you want to be accompanying this guy up to his room? He's pretty gruff. Unless you're into that sort of thing."

Logan growls at Wyatt. "I'm inviting her up for dinner."

"You cook?" Wyatt's eyes widen. "Wow. My apologies, Cali. I hope you ate a late snack."

The elevator doors ding open, and Logan mutters, "That couldn't come soon enough."

Wyatt pretends not to have heard him. "Have fun, you two, and if you get bored with the old grump, I'll be downstairs at the bar."

The younger brother shuffles out, winks at me, and the doors close.

"I'll kill him," Logan grumbles under his breath.

I smile, staring up at Logan. "Why? He was just being friendly."

"He was trying to get in your pants," he says, matter of fact, and straightens his shoulders. He tilts his neck to one side, cracking it and releasing quite a bit of tension.

"And that's a problem, why?" I ask, a faint smile on my lips.

He lowers his head, his gaze locked on me. "If you're looking for a one-night stand, he's the guy for it. But don't expect anything else from him. Ever."

The elevator reaches the penthouse suite, and the doors open directly to his room. "Are you coming?" he asks, glancing at me over his shoulder. "Unless you prefer to get laid with no strings attached tonight. Wyatt is the man to push all your buttons."

He seems to do an excellent job of pushing my buttons, though not necessarily the same ones. "You don't like your brother," I say.

"I have nothing against Wyatt. Just the fact he doesn't believe in commitment."

"And you do?" I glance down at his left hand. It's absent of a ring, which is good since I'm up in his penthouse suite. "Is there a Mrs. Logan Henderson?"

"No." He's quick to answer and shoot down any further conversation on the matter. "That topic is closed for discussion."

FIVE

Logan

CALI IS QUITE A CHATTERBOX. Worse than Julianna while she was growing up.

I refuse to discuss my divorce with her. It's none of her business that my ex-wife, Jess, left me for another man.

It was a real blow to my ego, opening the door and witnessing my best friend shacking up with my wife.

Now, he's my ex-best friend, and she's my ex-wife.

I don't know and don't care whether the two of them are together. Julianna knows not to discuss it with me. She visits her mother once a month, sometimes twice a month, if there's a holiday or birthday to celebrate.

But Jess is back in New York City, where we lived before moving to Montana. It's quite a change of pace.

"Make yourself comfortable. You should probably sit." I gesture to the sofa. I don't need Cali tripping over her feet again.

And while she's insisted that she's doing fine, the doctor cleared her, and there's nothing to worry about, I get the nagging feeling that she's hiding something from me.

I intend to get it out of her before the night is over.

Maybe I can help. If she needs to see a specialist and can't afford it or requires grossly overpriced medication, I can help tip the scale in her favor.

Cali doesn't listen. Why would I think that she might spend ten seconds following instructions? The girl is a wild spirit, carefree and bubbly.

We are nothing alike.

That's not to say I don't admire that innocence, but she's still young. Twenty-nine is practically a baby when I look back and remember the crazy things I did in my twenties.

I just turned forty-three, and I swear I'm a different person than I was fourteen years ago. For starters, I was a new father with a one-year-old daughter.

Now I'm a grumpy old man. It comes with being a single father, getting cheated on, and raising a teenage daughter by myself.

I grab a few fresh ingredients from the fridge and take out a giant pot to boil water. "Is there anything that you're allergic to?" I ask.

Cali shakes her head. "No, but I don't like cheese."

"Noted," I say with a wry grin. "I'll make us pasta, but no cheese on yours."

"Thank you." She pulls the stool out from the counter and sits on it while she watches me cook.

"Do you drink wine?"

"I'd love a glass," Cali says, and climbs down from the stool. "If you point me in the direction, I can grab us each a glass."

I open the cabinet and reach for the wine glasses on the top shelf. She'd never be able to reach without climbing on a chair, and that's entirely out of the question.

"There's a bottle of red on the counter and a corkscrew in the drawer beneath it." I gesture toward the wine bottle display. There are only a few bottles out. Most are kept in the basement cellar beneath the lodge.

Cali pops the cork and pours each of us a glass.

I inhale the fragrant aroma before taking a sip. The taste is exquisite. That's what five hundred dollars a bottle will get you. I have a case in the wine cellar. Most of it is reserved for special guests and when I entertain, which hasn't happened since the divorce.

My closest friend, the one who didn't screw me over, Levi Luxenberg, is back in New York City. Not that he can't visit, but he's busy with his daughter and his fiancée. The man is quite upstanding. When he learned that he had a five-year-old daughter and she had no one after her mother's death, he jumped on a plane and brought her home. The nanny too.

When I get settled with the lodge, I have plans to bring them out to explore the slopes. They ought to teach the kid when she's old enough to ski or snowboard.

Perhaps Julianna can teach Amelia.

"We should have done a toast," Cali says as she sips the wine. "Wow. This stuff is divine."

"Yeah, that's what five hundred a bottle gets you. Divine," I repeat with a smile.

She coughs on my remark, her eyes wide, and she puts the glass on the counter.

"You don't like it?" I ask, glancing at her over my shoulder. "You can open a different bottle if it's too dry for you."

"No, it's perfect. It's expensive. I don't want to waste a sip before our meal."

I wave my hand dismissively. "It's fine. I have another case of that stuff in the wine cellar downstairs."

Cali watches from the counter while I chop the vegetables and dice up the tomatoes, making my homemade spaghetti sauce.

"Where'd you learn to cook?" she asks.

I can't scold her for asking. It's a fair question, even if I don't want to discuss Jess. "My ex never cooked, and I wanted Julianna to eat a proper meal that was healthy and nutritious. Which meant I had to learn."

"Recently divorced?" she asks.

I'm sure she can Google it if she's curious. Her phone isn't out. She's being polite at least, which I appreciate.

"Yes. I'd prefer not to talk about it."

"Fair enough." Cali forces a smile, and she takes another sip of the wine before resting the glass and her hands on the counter. "I'm not much of a cook. I mean, I can boil water and make jarred spaghetti sauce, but following a recipe is my downfall. I glance at the sheet, and there are too many instructions, and it gets overwhelming."

"That's how Julianna is when I tell her to help with dinner. I can read her the recipe, but if she has to read it, it's like she's staring at a foreign language."

"Yes!" she exclaims. "You get it."

I don't get it, but I've heard my daughter complain enough about cooking that I managed to create a system where she helps, and we both prepare dinner.

Although we haven't had to do that since the lodge reopened after renovations, and for a while, I had a private chef preparing our meals while I was going through the divorce. When it was finalized, I didn't want to get rid of Damien, so I hired him to run the kitchen at the restaurant in the lodge.

We went from being a place to eat at the lodge to being the hottest place in town. Not that the town of Breckenridge is huge, but we stole a bit of business from the other joints in town.

There's always a wait, even on weeknights off-season. Reservations are recommended.

"Are you any better with dessert?" I ask, glancing at Cali over my shoulder.

She sits propped on the stool, and I swear if she falls off, I'll never forgive myself for buying those chairs.

"I'm good at eating it."

I chuckle. "Come here, taste my sauce." I stir the concoction, and she slides off the stool, eyebrow raised.

"That sounds dirty, Mr. Henderson."

"Call me Logan." I let her taste the red sauce with the wooden spoon.

She blows on it for a second before bringing it to her lips. Her eyes close, and she presses her lips together with a slight moan. "Gosh, that's amazing."

"You like my sauce?" I say with a smirk. I'm all about innuendo, and this woman is making me hard, watching her tongue swipe across her lips. Her cheeks are rosy and her pupils dark.

"Yes, I'd die for another taste."

"How is it? Is the sauce too salty?"

"Not at all. It's perfect. You know how to cook."

Why does she seem surprised by that fact? I grab the bowls and dish the pasta first, letting her put however much sauce and meat she wants on her meal.

We bring the dishes to the small wooden table in the kitchen. The table expands, but Julianna and I eat downstairs most nights, so there's been no reason to extend it.

Dinner is pleasant, with polite chit-chat but nothing too intimate or personal. She strays from asking questions about my divorce or daughter, and I do the same, not wanting to overstep any boundaries.

I invited her for a nice meal, not to convince her to sleep with me. Besides, that door is shut. After Jess cheated on me, trusting women again isn't easy.

By the end of dinner, we've demolished the exquisite bottle of wine, and I clear the dishes, rinsing them before putting them into the dishwasher.

"You're going to make dessert, right?" I joke.

"That depends. Do you have a box of brownie mix in the pantry?"

The elevator dings, and Julianna and Izzie come waltzing into the penthouse. "Hi, Dad. Cali!" Julianna squeals, excited to see who I've brought home. My daughter's eyes widen. "OMG, are you on a date, Dad?"

I never get used to her saying her text speak aloud. "I promised I'd take care of dinner for Cali if she went to the in-house physician."

"You made her visit Dr. Reynolds?" Julianna's face scrunches. "He's hotter than you, Dad."

"Gee, thanks, kiddo." I splash her with water, and she shrieks like she's melting. My kid is all drama. I'm surprised she didn't try out for drama club in high school.

"Your daughter is right. Dr. Reynolds is easy on the eyes," Cali says. She wiggles her eyebrows. "Is he married?"

"No," I say, and shake my head. "But you're not his type."

"What's that mean?" Cali asks.

"That's harsh, *Old Man*, even for you," Julianna says.

"Old Man?" I glare at my daughter. I'm not the least bit angry, just perturbed that she'd call me that in front of Cali, no less. "And he's not interested in women nearly half his age," I say, pinning Cali with my stare.

"I'm twenty-nine," she says, like that somehow makes it better.

"Dad," Julianna interrupts us yet again. "Can Izzie spend the night?"

"Izzie needs to ask her parents, but it's fine with me." I'm glad to see Julianna spend time with a friend outside school.

Julianna and Izzie head toward the elevator. They're not done exploring the lodge or may not want to be around any parents. I'm okay with that as well. I like the thought of having Cali alone, to myself.

Once the girls are gone, it's just Cali and me, alone.

"I was joking earlier about liking Dr. Reynolds," she says.

I'm unsure why she feels it necessary to explain herself, but I let her ramble on because it's endearing to listen to her speak.

"Were you?"

"He is easy on the eyes, but he's not my type." She lets that thought linger a little too long.

"What is your type?" I ask. I shouldn't. I should open up a bottle of water, not another bottle of red. I'm pouring us each a glass while I mix the ingredients to make brownies.

Cali is right beside me, her back against the counter. I'm not sure if it's holding her up or if she's steady on her feet. Either way, at least she won't be driving anywhere tonight.

It's a dangerous game, flirting with a girl bound to break my heart. The woman I loved had destroyed me. Why wouldn't a woman whom I barely know?

"Tall, dark, handsome." She smirks, glancing me up and down. "A man who knows what he wants, is kind and considerate and isn't afraid to speak his mind. Even if it means a disagreement."

I stew on her words. I'm not sure I fit into the 'kind and considerate' category, but the rest is easily me.

"What about you?" Cali asks. "What's your type?"

I turn the oven on and wait for it to preheat.

"My type?" I ask, and fold my arms across my chest, my back against the counter as I mull over her words. "A woman who doesn't cheat. That's honest, even if it's brutally painful to hear."

I don't have much else on the list right now. Jess had met all my mental boxes on the imaginary checklist for girlfriend and eventually wife. But it didn't matter, because she managed to screw me over, but not before screwing that numb-nuts.

"I'm sorry she hurt you," Cali says, her voice soft, and she sounds genuine and sincere.

"Yeah, I don't want to talk about it." I down the glass of red and pour another, filling the glass. It doesn't matter if I get tipsy or fully drunk. This is my house and my lodge. I can do whatever the hell I damn well please.

"Understood." Cali rests a hand on my arm.

Her touch is warm and comforting and radiates a tingle of heat throughout my body. She stirs a flame that I thought was dead inside of me and could never be rekindled.

She steps closer, closing the distance, and her hand rests on my arm, the other on my chest. Cali leans on her tiptoes.

I know what's coming, and I don't stop her.

She kisses me, her breath soft and warm. Her lips are smooth and sweet. She tastes like fresh cherries.

I open my mouth to deepen the kiss, but my brain keeps replaying the horrible things that Jess did to me, and I pull away.

"You should go," I say.

"But we haven't had dessert yet."

I turn off the oven, making it apparent that dinner is done. There will be no dessert. She ruined it by crossing the line and kissing me.

I walk toward the elevator, and she sighs, following several feet behind me. I press the button, wanting it to be here already.

The tension in the room is thick.

Cali is breathing heavily from the kiss, or maybe my abrupt nature has her flustered. But I can't go down that road with her. Not now and likely not ever.

I'm a man too far damaged for repair. She doesn't deserve me and all the baggage that comes with me.

The elevator doors ding open, and Cali steps inside.

"Goodnight," I say roughly, and her eyes tighten. She doesn't say anything. Not even a thank you for dinner.

She's biting her bottom lip, and I swear if she cries, I won't be able to contain myself. Cali doesn't get to cry. She wasn't the one who was ripped apart and torn to shreds by the one person who vowed to be with me through all of it.

Logically, I recognize it's not Cali's fault. But I can't separate the two tonight.

The doors shut, and I breathe a sigh of relief that she's gone.

SIX

Cali

WHAT THE HELL JUST HAPPENED? My head spins, and my eyes burn.

I lean back against the elevator, not pressing any buttons.

I can't remember what floor my room is on. Everything inside of me aches.

I hit the button for the lobby, and the elevator car takes me down to the first floor. I stalk out, heading straight for the bar.

While I could go to bed, a drink sounds better. I walk into the bar. There are a few patrons, but it's not overly crowded. Most of the lodge is family oriented. The bar is the exception.

I grab a seat at the counter and order a Long Island iced tea. It's sweet enough, but it will pack a punch. Plus, I've already had my fair share of expensive wine upstairs.

That's probably the reason I stupidly leaned in and kissed Logan Henderson. I didn't realize he'd freak out when I locked lips with him.

Was kissing me that awful?

"Cali, right?" Wyatt asks. He strolls up from the opposite side of the bar where he'd been playing darts.

"Yes," I say. I don't give him much else.

He glances me over as the bartender brings my drink over to me. "Thanks," I say, and Wyatt gestures toward the alcoholic beverage.

"Put it on my tab. And I'll have another round."

"I can buy my drinks," I snap at him.

"I'm sure you can, but I was being a gentleman." Wyatt smiles and leans back against the bar. His thumbs hook on the belt loops in his jeans.

He's handsome, and the longer I stare at him, I can see the resemblance between the two brothers.

"Teach your brother to be a gentleman," I mutter, gulping down my drink.

Wyatt shifts sideways to face me and eventually takes the empty seat next to me. Perhaps he realizes it's going to be a long night. "He usually is the gentleman. What'd he do?"

"He kicked me out, sent me into the elevator because I kissed him. Heaven forbid my lips to touch his."

Wyatt cracks a grin. "You kissed my brother? Good for you."

"Yeah, not good for me. Did you hear what I said? He kicked me out."

Wyatt's brow pinches, and he runs a hand through his hair. "He probably freaked out."

"From a kiss? The guy's forty-something. He's not a virgin," I say. How can he possibly be freaked out from one simple kiss? I didn't even get to explore his mouth with my tongue.

"He's been married since he was nineteen to the same woman. His first and only love. The man doesn't have much experience outside his ex-wife." Wyatt chuckles. "And he'd murder me if he knew I was telling you this."

"Yeah, I'll bet." I down the rest of my drink and gesture to the bartender for another. "He acts like it's a crime for me to have feelings for him. I shouldn't like him. I want to hate him," I say, and my nose twitches.

"But?"

"But he's gorgeous. Have you seen your brother? Not to mention how kind and caring he can be when he's not acting like a jerk. He carried me to dinner the other night when I hurt my ankle, and earlier today, he carried me to the in-house physician."

"That doesn't sound like Logan, carrying guests around the lodge." Wyatt chuckles and sips his beer. "Don't get me wrong. My brother likes you. It's obvious. He doesn't invite anyone up into his home, ever. He's just not great with getting in touch with his feelings and shit."

I don't believe Wyatt. "He doesn't like me."

"I'll bet the next round that he likes you," Wyatt says.

"How are you going to prove it?"

Wyatt smirks and waves at Logan as he storms into the bar. His eyes widen when he sees me, and then he glances at Wyatt.

Heat emanates from Logan like he's a fierce inferno raging and about ready to burst. Logan snarls and lunges at Wyatt, grabbing him by the lapels and yanking him off the barstool. "You haven't changed one bit," Logan seethes between clenched teeth.

"Neither have you," Wyatt says, remaining far calmer than one should be, given the fact he's about to be assaulted.

But they're brothers, and maybe Wyatt knows how to calm his hot-headed brother down.

"I can't believe you, trying to steal Cali like you tried to steal Jess all those years ago!" Logan's eyes are wide. He doesn't even notice that I'm on the stool, right next to him.

I rest my hand on his arm, trying to soothe his insecurities and reassure him that whatever he thinks this is, it isn't.

You can't cheat on someone when you're not in a relationship with them.

"Your brother didn't steal me," I interject. "I'm not an object to be owned." I grab my drink and toss it in Logan's face to cool him off.

"Have you had your fun yet?" He lifts me from the ground, putting me over his shoulder and carrying me out of the bar, caveman style.

"Logan, put me down!" I shriek, and he relents outside of the lodge's bar.

"What was that?" He folds his arms across his chest. His biceps bulge and flex. He's pissed, and I didn't even do anything wrong.

"Me, having a nice conversation with your brother. Stop acting like an ass." I walk away from him, but he grabs my arm and spins me around in his grasp to face him.

"We're not done, *Sunshine*."

"Okay, but if we're giving nicknames, you're a *Mountain Grump*."

"Real mature," Logan says. He glances me over, his lips pressed together, but he doesn't say anything.

His silence is overwhelming.

"Listen, I don't know what happened between you and your ex-wife," I say, although I have a pretty good idea of what Wyatt told me and what Logan is looking for in a partner. "But I'm not her. I don't cheat. I never have and never will. Wyatt, your brother, was having a drink with me because I sat alone at the bar."

"He was hitting on you," Logan says. "He hits on all the pretty girls who come to the bar alone."

It doesn't matter whether he was hitting on me or not. I wasn't going home with him. "Even if you don't trust your brother, at least give me a little more credit."

"I don't know you."

He's right. He doesn't know me. We don't know much about each other. "Exactly. Why do you care who I talk to or share a drink with if you don't even know me or care about me?"

"That's where you're wrong, Cali," he says, taking a step closer. He invades my personal space.

His scent is intoxicating. His breath is hot and warm, and my body tingles from our proximity. I want to kiss him, but that didn't go over well upstairs in his place. I don't need another repeat performance of him kicking me out. Although, this time, would he kick me out entirely of his resort or just demand that I go to my room like a child?

"Then correct me," I say, my gaze meeting his, never wavering.

His stare is intense.

It's hot, and my breathing grows louder and thicker.

He leans forward, and I swear he's going to kiss me. But he doesn't. His breath mingles with mine. His eyes remain locked on me like I'm the center of his world and nothing else exists.

"I do care about you, more than I should." His words are like honey, and my insides tingle all over. "But you are practically a child. Sleeping with my brother will only end up hurting you."

"I don't want to sleep with your brother!" Why can't he get it into his thick skull that the only man I have eyes for is him, Logan Henderson?

He shakes his head. "I don't believe you. I saw the two of you laughing and having a grand ole time before I stepped foot in the bar."

"It's a crime for me to have fun with another man when I'm not even dating anyone?" I quip.

Logan shuts his mouth.

I expect him to yell, scream, tell me that I'm like his ex, and that he'll never trust me again. But instead, he turns and walks away, leaving me standing there even more dumbfounded and confused.

Did Wyatt sleep with Jess? He'd mentioned a friend, not his brother.

Logan storms off down the hallway, and I wait a minute before deciding whether it's safe to return to the bar or if I should just call it a night and go upstairs.

While I'm still standing awkwardly outside the entrance, Wyatt stalks up to me, beer bottle in hand. "I guess you two didn't make up," Wyatt says, noticing that his brother left me standing there in the cold, alone.

"He thinks I want to sleep with you."

"Do you?" Wyatt asks, his gaze latched on mine, waiting for an answer.

I'm not looking for a winter fling, or any fling, for that matter. I usually fall hard and fast. Maybe that's what's happening with Logan, at least for me.

I rub my forehead. "No, I like your grumpy brother."

"He is grumpy," Wyatt says, and quirks a grin.

"Did you sleep with Logan's ex?" I ask, still not understanding the dynamics or drama. Logan has some unresolved issues with his brother regarding his ex-wife.

"No, but years ago, Logan caught his wife making a pass at me. She was drunk, we were all on vacation together, and I tried to smooth things over by pretending that I was the one interested and that she had no desire to be with me and only wanted him."

"Seems her eye wandered, and it wasn't only with you," I say. That should have been a sign, a red flag.

"Exactly," Wyatt says, pointing at me. "You get it. Logan, well, he never did. He blamed me back then for what happened with Jess, and when she brought another man into his bed, he's been a major pain in the ass ever since."

"Love does strange things to people," I say.

"Are you speaking from experience?" Wyatt asks.

"I plead the fifth."

———

I spend the next few days avoiding Logan while trying to get as much work done as possible. I set up a few locations for video shoots to get footage of guests going down the slopes, the lodge, the restaurants, and the bar.

But I still haven't gotten my interview with Logan, and it doesn't seem like I'm going to at this point. Maybe I should let it go.

I only have forty-eight more hours on the company's dime before I have to fly home to sunny LA. I look forward to the sun. Even though it's winter, it's warmer down south, and there's zero chance of snow. My kind of weather.

Most of my video shoots have been aesthetic.

"Cali!" Jules waves to me as she runs down the hallway, catching up. I have my phone out, near the window, trying to capture as much light as possible. My ring light died hours ago and is recharging.

"Sorry I bailed on you this week. Can I help?"

"I'm just shooting some footage," I say.

"That's my favorite part. Did you get anything from the ski lift?"

"I didn't. Do you want to come with me?"

Her eyes light up. "I would love to. Should we grab our jackets and meet back here in ten minutes?"

I head upstairs to grab my coat and an extra set of warm clothes. The boots are nice and toasty, and it's frigid outside, so I don't want to shiver and shake the camera when I shoot a video.

I slip on my gloves and head down. Jules is already waiting for me.

She grabs my hand and drags me to the ski lift. I have no clue where I'm going, but I could have just as easily followed the signs, although I hadn't spent too much time outdoors.

"How's your ankle?" Jules asks as we step in front of the ski lift and are hoisted into the chair. The bar loosely comes down. I scoot back and turn my camera on, sliding to video footage to get pictures of the slopes and guests enjoying the winter wonderland.

"Better," I say. The audio will all be cut, so it doesn't matter that we're talking over the footage I take.

"You should go down the slopes. I mean, how will you review it and give a fair rating if you've never been down?"

She's right. "When we get back, how about you show me the ropes and come with me?"

"Okay," Jules says, her smile wide and full of excitement.

I snap dozens of pictures and take even more footage for the vlog. The review I'll write will showcase specific elements of the lodge: dining, hotel, and entertainment. It also focuses on comfort, quality for the price, and what makes them different than any other similar venue.

What makes Blue Sky Resort different is the grumpy owner, but I don't think that's what the viewers want to see. Or maybe they do? But I'm not about to trash his name, even if he did run me out of his penthouse suite after I kissed him.

Who cares if he's not into me? I certainly don't.

In less than two days, I'll be gone and will never have to look at that jerk again.

"Are you going to give us a five-star review?" Jules asks. The kid gets right to the point. "Dad will be devastated if you write about the cranky owner."

That wins a smile. "Your dad is very cranky," I say.

"Worse than a toddler." Jules points down below at the black bears trudging through the snow. "Look!"

"Oh wow! Are the skiers in any danger?" I try to hold my phone steady as I shoot video footage from high above.

"They shouldn't be. The bears are on the other side of the mountain pass. The slopes are behind us," Jules says. She's quite familiar with the trails and the route we're taking. "Besides, they're not grizzlies, so it should be fine."

I breathe a sigh of relief. We pass by the bears and jump off when we get back to where we started.

"Come on, let's get you some equipment, and we can go skiing together." Jules grabs my hand and drags me inside. She's lit up like a Christmas tree and practically glowing.

"It's okay with your dad if you go out?" I ask. He already hates me, although I'm not sure what I did wrong to deserve his wrath. Was it because I kissed him or had a drink in the bar and his brother showed up?

Maybe a little of both?

We've done a decent job of avoiding each other. I can't complain. He's made the rest of my week dull in comparison, but that's all right with me.

Jules hurries behind the counter. "What size do you wear?"

"Eight."

She grabs two pairs of boots and hands me the size eights. "Strap those on, and we'll grab skis next. Also, helmets." She grabs two helmets from the rack and hands me one.

It's not pretty, but it's functional, which is all that matters. I make sure the helmet is secure and tight, following her outside. We grab a set of skis and poles. Jules shows me how to secure my boot to the ski and gives me a quick mini-lesson out front on the snow.

To say that I don't grasp it quickly is an understatement.

"You'll get the hang of it," Jules insists.

"Maybe I should try a class first."

"It's fine. We'll go on the bunny hills." She helps me toward the ski lift, and I can't help but have a sinking feeling in the pit of my stomach.

Is it nervousness?

Or maybe I know I'm not cut out to be on skis, and this is the worst idea imaginable. It wasn't like Jules had to do much to talk me into trying it.

I forge onward because, let's face it, this kid is fifteen and has no fear. Do I want her to think I'm a coward? Hell, no.

And I like her dad, even if he's a grumpy mountain man who owns a ski lodge. I want to see what all the fuss is about, why people come here from all over the world.

Did I mention I'm not much of a winter girl?

My fingers are chilly, but the ski boots are warmer than the cozy ones I left inside the lodge.

The bench sways, rocking back and forth as we sit back on the chair lift. The bar loosely keeps us in place from falling. I remove my gloves, wanting to get a better handle on the ski pole, when my glove flies over the edge with my pole and phone.

Shit.

Without thinking, I lunge for it, knocking the bar loose, and in a flash, I'm falling from the lift into the thicket of snow below.

I hit the ground with a thud, but it's not flat. There's an incline, and I tumble down, skis on and all.

I should have tried snowboarding instead.

My hand is frozen from the ice. Numb.

One pole is way above where I fell.

The other is halfway down the hillside, where I crashed ungracefully. And my phone, I don't have a clue where that or my glove landed.

When I finally hit the bottom, I realize I'm between mountains and trees. My ankle is no longer the problem. Everything hurts, like my body is on fire.

Groaning, it takes a minute for me to regroup after having the wind knocked out of me.

I glance up, and Jules stares at me as the ride continues, and she's too far away to do anything.

"I'll get help!" she shouts. "Stay there!"

Yeah, where else am I going to go?

SEVEN

Logan

JULIANNA COMES RUNNING into my office. She has her helmet and ski boots on, but the rest of the equipment isn't attached.

My daughter is out of breath, but her energy has me looking up and concerned.

"What is it?" I ask.

It's not uncommon for a guest to get injured on the slopes. We make everyone sign a liability waiver before going out onto the trails.

But why is Julianna rushing in here like it's the end of the world? I didn't even realize she was going out skiing this afternoon.

"It's Cali," she says, gasping for breath. Her cheeks are red, and she gestures for me to follow.

"What do you mean?" The gruffness in my voice can't be hidden away or contained. What the hell did Cali do this time?

"She wanted to go skiing and fell off the chair lift."

"Of course she did," I mutter, and rub my forehead. I slip into my winter boots and grab a jacket, heading outside with Cali on my tail.

"Do you know if she was hurt?" I ask.

"She fell hard and then rolled down the hill. But she was still conscious."

"That's good." At least the part where she was still conscious. "Why the hell was she on the slopes?" I head for the emergency equipment and grab a snowmobile with a sledding stretcher attached.

I grab a radio and communicate that one of our guests is likely injured and we need additional units out searching for her.

Julianna climbs onto the back, and I pull away, heading in the direction she instructs. "How the hell did she fall off?" I ask. The metal bar is supposed to keep any guests from falling over the edge.

"I don't know. Her glove went over the edge and then her pole. The next thing I knew, she wasn't seated next to me, and the chair was swinging like crazy. I was trying to hold on so I wouldn't fall next."

"I told her that she couldn't go on the slopes! Dammit!" I shout, and press the gas harder, trying to get to Cali as quickly as possible.

Why couldn't she listen to me?

The cold sting of the air and the wind from riding the snowmobile burn my cheeks. I'm not dressed for a snow rescue. And while I requested our ski patrol to help, they also have to keep an eye on the guests on the slopes.

The farther we get from the lodge, the colder every inch of my body feels. In the distance, I catch a glimpse of her dark hair against the snow. The sun is beginning to go down behind the mountains, and I radio in our location for assistance.

I slow the engine beside her and climb off the snowmobile.

Cali grimaces and shoots my daughter a look. "You called *him* for help?"

I'm not happy about it, either. Why the hell was Cali on the ski slopes? She injured her ankle a few days ago and kept falling. What made her think this was a good idea?

I bend to Cali's level, and Julianna grabs the first aid kit off the stretcher. "Grab me a penlight," I instruct my daughter.

She unzips the bag and hands it to me. I flip it on and point it at Cali's eyes, wanting to ensure she doesn't have a concussion or any permanent brain injury. Her pupils react normally. That's a good sign.

"Can you wiggle your toes for me?"

"I can stand, but my knee hurts," Cali says. "And my ankle isn't doing me any favors, either."

"Don't stand." I don't want to risk any further injuries. "I have a crew that's on their way. We're going to get you loaded onto that stretcher and take you back to Dr. Reynolds to examine you."

As soon as the ski patrol team arrives, they slide her onto the stretcher, strap her in, and cocoon her in a blanket to make sure she doesn't go into shock or get frostbite from the cold.

I drive the snowmobile back, taking my time, since Cali is attached. I don't trust anyone else to the task. Once I arrive outside the medical building, she's carried in on the stretcher.

Not being able to go in with her, I wait outside. Julianna's eyes are red, but I'm sure it's from the cold.

"Go inside, get ready for dinner," I say.

"I'm not hungry."

Neither am I.

I can't help but worry about Cali and how she's doing.

"It's all my fault." Her eyes fill with tears.

"What is?" I ask, pulling her in for a hug.

"Cali wouldn't have gone skiing if I didn't talk her into it. It's my fault she's hurt."

I rub Julianna's back and bring her inside the waiting room area of the clinic. At least it's warm inside. I may not deserve the warmth, but my daughter doesn't need to suffer because of the things I said that hurt Cali.

"This isn't your fault. It was an accident," I say. "You should get dinner. You can call up Izzie and see if she'd like to join you."

"She has plans. I'll wait here. I want to see Cali."

I sit on the hard plastic chair. "Me too," I say.

"You're not going to give her a hard time when you see her." Julianna slips off her coat, hands me the jacket, and folds her arms across her chest.

I shove her jacket back at her. "Go put this away."

She groans and rolls her eyes. "Fine. But I'm going to freeze in the atrium."

"You'll survive for five minutes."

She huffs and hurries out of the clinic to the main lodge. She's not in the atrium for more than a few seconds, hightailing it as quickly as possible.

Silence fills the room, and eventually, Cali emerges from the back with a set of crutches.

This can't go over well. The girl can barely walk on two feet, and she's got crutches?

"Just a sprained ankle and bruised knee," Cali says. "Doctor says I'm lucky I didn't break a bone."

"And the crutches are for—"

"Stability, so that I can get from one side of the lodge to the other. And you don't have to carry me." She grins cheekily.

My cock twitches in my jeans at the memory of carrying her. I clear my throat, needing a distraction. The frigid temperatures outside should do it. "Are you ready?" I ask, opening the door.

Cali winces from the chill and then hobbles, using the crutches through the atrium. It takes her longer than it should. She's not great on them, and to say I'm not concerned is an understatement.

I keep waiting for her to tip over, and for me to leap in to catch her.

I grab the door to the lodge, holding it open for her as she makes it slowly inside.

"Cali!" Julianna squeals, and comes running from down the hallway toward us.

"Hey," Cali says, and gives a warm smile. "Thanks for bringing help."

"Even if it was the cranky old man?" Julianna quips.

"I'm right here," I say, waving my hand in front of them. They're acting as if I were invisible, talking about me right in front of me.

"Do you hear anyone talking?" Cali jokes.

I groan and roll my eyes. "You two can get dinner together."

Cali grabs my arm, linking ours together. "Thank you for saving my life."

I'd say she's being a little overdramatic, except she could have frozen to death if my daughter hadn't been with her and gotten help. "You're welcome. How about we all grab dinner together?"

Cali forces a smile and tugs her bottom lip between her teeth. I can't tell if she's nervous or hesitant. "I'm just going to head up to my room. It's been a long day."

"You need to eat," I say. "Especially if the doctor gave you any type of painkillers."

"Just ibuprofen. He didn't give me any of the good stuff," she jokes.

I glare at her. "Drugs aren't a joking matter." I turn my attention to Julianna, wanting her to get the message as well.

"Got it, Dad. Gosh, you're so lame sometimes." Julianna walks on one side of me while Cali hobbles on the crutches on the other.

I want to help Cali. Hell, I'd carry her all through the lodge if it meant her not getting hurt the rest of the time that she's here. But I doubt she'd let me do that for her.

I ignore my daughter's remark. "How long are you in town?" I ask, keeping a slow pace beside Cali as we approach the restaurant. Tonight, I'm not cooking for her. The last time I invited her up to the penthouse, she got the wrong idea about us.

Not that it was entirely her fault. I did give her mixed signals, indicating that I was interested in her. Because I was interested, I couldn't turn off the signals even if my life depended on it.

I'll do better tonight. Keep things professional between us. After all, she's here on business, and I don't want to muddy her review for the resort.

"I leave the day after tomorrow."

"What about your phone?" Julianna asks. "We didn't recover it when you fell off the ski lift."

"It's fine. All the footage should have been backed up to the cloud. I can access it when I get home. Although I need to check in with my boss and let her know that I'm not ignoring her texts."

"You can use my phone," I offer.

After we get seated at our private table in the back, Cali slips into the booth, and I sit across from her with my daughter. The waitress hands all of us menus. I already know what I want, and Julianna doesn't even glance at the menu.

We've eaten here enough times to know what's good and what's amazing. Nothing is bad. Ever.

We put in our orders, and I request a bottle of white wine for the table along with two glasses. Julianna isn't getting any alcohol until she's twenty-one.

The waitress returns with two glasses and pops the cork, letting me smell it before pouring us each a glass.

"Can I have a sip?" my daughter asks.

"You know the rules." I can't risk our restaurant losing its liquor license for serving underage minors.

I take a sip. The alcohol is sweet and fragrant and not the least bit bitter. There's no burning sensation like with cheap wine.

I retrieve my cell phone from my pants pocket and unlock it before handing it to Cali. "I hope you remember her number."

"I swear it spells devil," Cali quips with a laugh. She opens the messages section and begins typing. There's a soft sigh, and then she glances up at me before continuing typing her message and hitting send. "I didn't realize that you know Bridget Lancaster."

The name brings a bitter metallic taste to my lips. "Are you going through my contacts?" I reach for my phone.

"No, but her name popped up when I typed in her phone number. Bridget is my boss."

My stomach tenses, and my hands bunch into fists. "I'll take my phone back now," I growl at her, and snatch the device from her fingers.

"Ex-girlfriend?" Cali guesses based on my sudden shift in mood.

"No. Although that woman tried to ruin my marriage."

"How?" Julianna's eyes light up as she scoots forward, wanting all the dirty details.

That's not a conversation to be had in front of my fifteen-year-old daughter. "We're not discussing *Bridget*," I say with a sneer. "That woman has been nothing but a menace."

That sick, sinking feeling in the pit of my stomach won't disappear. Is that why Cali is here? To destroy my reputation and the business I just helped turn around and get off the ground?

Blue Sky Resort had its share of problems over the past decade, with a hostage situation among one of the worst incidents. But I believed I could turn the place around and breathe new life into it. Was I wrong?

"Well, I can assure you, Mr. Henderson, that my video review will be honest and genuine. Whatever bad blood is between you and Bridget, it will not be reflected in the final product."

I want to be relieved, but I can't. Not until I see what's put out for the world to view.

"I appreciate that, and for the umpteenth time, please call me Logan."

"Of course," she says, and her cheeks redden.

Dinner is brought to the table, and Julianna doesn't so much as touch her food. She keeps glancing between Cali and me.

"Dad, is it okay if I take my dinner upstairs?" Julianna asks.

Is something wrong? Is she not feeling well? "Why?" I ask.

"The sexual tension between the two of you is palpable. I know you're angry with what Mom did," Julianna says, staring at me. "But Cali is cute, and as far as I know, she's single. Enjoy your night together. Just don't stay out past curfew."

Before I can tell my daughter to sit her ass back down and demand she keep me company, the kid grabs her plate and silverware, hightailing it out of the restaurant.

"I think we just got set up on a date," Cali says. Her tongue darts out and licks the corner of her lips. She places her fork down on the table.

"Is something wrong with your meal?"

"No, I just—I can ask the waitress to box it and take it back to my room."

I take a bite of the Chilean Seabass, and the homemade sauce drizzled on top is absolutely astounding. The chef outdid himself again.

"Why would you do that?" I ask, glancing up at Cali. "Just because my daughter bailed doesn't mean that you have to leave. Besides, I doubt you can carry your food and manage the crutches up to your room."

Her eyes narrow. She knows I'm right. "I was trying not to make this any more awkward than it already is," Cali says.

"Why's it awkward?" I take another bite and try the homemade garlic mashed potatoes.

"Other than you hate me?" She laughs nervously, and she avoids my stare as she picks at her food.

"Do you not like your meal?" I ask, commenting on her pushing food around her plate.

She forces a smile. "The meal isn't the problem."

"Then why aren't you eating?" I ignore her remark. I refuse to be the problem. I haven't done anything wrong. At least not today. I saved her ass outside in the cold and snow.

Cali sighs and takes a bite of mashed potatoes, trying to make a point. She moans at the first bite, and whatever stubbornness that's been latched on like a leech finally releases itself. "Gosh, that's good. Better than sex," she mutters, and takes another bite.

Her eyes close, and the moan she elicits makes my cock hard.

Is she riling me up on purpose?

Does she realize what she does, the power she has over me?

"I don't think any meal could be better than sex." I have to disagree with her.

I don't even want to like her. But for some reason, I'm drawn to her, unable to tear my gaze away or tell my melting heart to freeze back over.

It's like she's able to tear down the barrier by thawing the ice with the heat of her innocent smile.

But that's all that's innocent. The way she sucks on the fork and moans is practically orgasmic. Is she getting off or trying to make me rock hard?

Just listening to her moan and watching her body react makes me want to kiss her. But I shouldn't. She's here strictly on business. Cali isn't looking to get laid, and I don't do hookups. I'm not a one-night stand kind of guy. That's entirely Wyatt's territory.

Besides, my daughter is upstairs, and she doesn't need to witness or hear the filthy things that I'd do to Cali if I had her in my bed.

"I don't know, Logan. These potatoes are to die for."

For a moment, I'm waiting for her to laugh or to tell me she's kidding around. "We have the same potatoes," I say. Our meal is different, but I'm sure the garlic potatoes come from the same batch.

"And you still think sex is better?" She laughs and rubs her eyes, the tears surfacing. But at least she's not upset. She's laughing so hard that she's crying. "I'm sorry." She holds up her hand, trying to catch her breath.

"Why are you apologizing?"

"Because you think you're a king in bed," Cali says. Her cheeks are red, and she fans herself. "I'm telling you; no sex is better than this dinner."

"Is that a challenge?" I should keep my mouth shut. But the woman has a way of getting under my skin. Does she really think those potatoes are better than sex? She's either had really bad sex or never experienced orgasm after orgasm.

Either way, I'm confident I can change her mind.

"You don't do no-strings-attached sex," Cali says.

She's right, I don't. But for some reason, I don't feel like that's what this girl is looking for, either. She's been here a week, and we've spent more time together than I've spent with any other guest who wasn't invited here personally by me.

"I don't," I say, staring at her. "Is that a problem?"

Cali shrugs. "I leave in two days. And no offense, but I hate the cold."

She's making it clear she's not planning on coming back or staying here any longer. I should be upset, disappointed, distraught.

"I hate the summer heat," I say, pinning her with my stare.

The girl quirks a wry grin. "Is this your idea of foreplay, old man?"

"Old man?" I scoff, and want to lunge across the table. Instead, I stand and scoot around to the booth. She has her leg up, and I sit beside her, bringing my arm up around her shoulders protectively. "Maybe I should put you on my lap, little girl."

She elbows me in the stomach and leans back, wiggling her butt against my crotch. "I'm almost thirty." Cali's head dips back onto my shoulder, and my fingers grab her neck, tilting her head and pulling her lips to mine.

Our lips clash, and fingers fumble. I can't get enough of her. My heart is pounding against my ribcage, straining to break free.

"Fourteen years age difference," I mutter. Damn, that's almost the age of my daughter, except Cali isn't a child. She's a grown woman. Every inch of her is all woman, from the curve of her breasts down her body. She is absolutely perfect, and I want her to be all mine.

Fuck. The woman knows how to make me even harder.

As her tongue pushes inside of my mouth, deepening the kiss, exploring me, all I can think about is what it would feel like to have her under me, pumping my cock inside of her, listening to her moaning and screaming my name.

And where the hell are we going to go?

I can't take her back to my place. We could sneak off to her room and bang it out. Isn't that what near thirty-year-olds call it these days?

My fingers trail across her thighs, and I cup her pussy through the thick denim. She rocks into my palm, and I'm grateful the table hides what we're doing, because neither of us is completely discreet.

"Still prefer the meal over my touch?" I ask, pulling my hand away.

Cali whimpers in protest. She rests her forehead against mine, gasping for breath. "I want—I want you," she says, and her words are like music to my ears.

"Not until you finish your dinner. All of it," I warn. "You're going to need your strength."

She whimpers, and I pull away, enough to let her eat without choking. Sex and the rest of our foreplay have to wait. I watch her attentively as she scarfs down her meal, and then we leave. There's no check to deal with or tip to leave. I pay my staff handsomely already.

"Where to?" Cali asks as she steps out of the booth with her crutches.

"A room," I say, and sweep her off her feet. "Leave your crutches. I'll have someone bring them up to your room later." I carry her out of the restaurant and to the elevator.

"Your place or mine?"

"Yours. My daughter is upstairs, and I don't need her hearing you scream my name all night."

"Oh, but the guests next door get to listen to it?"

"At least they're not related," I say. I press the button with my elbow to go up. "What floor?"

"Twelve."

I hit the button for the twelfth floor and wait for the double doors to close.

"Were you playing me back there with the potatoes?" I ask. At this point, I no longer care, but I want to know the truth.

She shakes her head, her arms around my neck as she's cuddled against me. "You can put me down," Cali says.

"And take the chance that another man might sweep you off your feet? I think not."

Her fingers trail along my chest, and I growl, trying like hell to keep my concentration and focus on getting Cali to her room.

"Room number?" I need to know which way to go down the hallway.

"Twelve Twenty-Two."

I head to the right, and she's only four rooms down the hallway.

"Room key?" I ask, and put her down, leaning her against the back of the door so she can dig out her room card.

Her eyes widen, and she grimaces.

"Let me guess. It's buried in the snow with your phone."

"Probably."

There's a master key in my office, but it'll be quicker to go downstairs and have the staff register a new key to the room.

"Stay here," I grumble, and hurry down to the lobby to get two room cards registered and grab a condom from the front desk drawer.

In record time, I'm back up to the twelfth floor. "It took you long enough," Cali jokes. I'm just glad she hasn't changed her mind.

I hand her the room keys and let her unlock the door, inviting me inside. "Come on in, although I'm sure you know what the place looks like." She laughs and hobbles two steps before I sweep her off her feet.

"You're not going to reinjure your ankle or your knee," I say, carrying her to the bed. Gently, I place her down on the mattress, and she stares up at me with a wry grin. "What?"

"You're chivalrous. I thought that only happened in movies and books."

My fingers work her boots free. They're the ones that she borrowed and will have to return tomorrow to the lodge.

She undoes the button on her jeans and lifts her hips. I help her out of her clothes, eager to undress her. I want to ravish her, kiss over every inch of her perfect skin.

Cali grimaces when her jeans move down her knees. She has a fresh bruise from the fall, but the doctor already looked at her injuries.

I pause. Maybe we shouldn't be doing this tonight. "I should let you rest."

"Don't you dare," Cali seethes, and sits up and throws her legs over the edge of the bed, ready to chase after me. "Get back here, Logan. You promised to show me that sex was better than dinner."

"Oh, it is," I say. She can't convince me otherwise. "Are you sure that you're up for it?" I don't want to hurt her, and she's been through a lot already. I climb onto the bed, straddling her hips.

I lean down, covering her lips with mine, greedily stealing a taste. She's warm beneath me, and I inch her shirt up, lifting it over her head and tossing it to the floor.

"How come I'm naked, and you still have all your clothes on?"

"You're not completely naked," I say. Cali's still wearing her panties and bra, although if it were up to me, I'd tear them right off.

Her fingernails trail along my stomach and loosen the button on my jeans. She inches the zipper down, and her hand goes right for the kill.

I grab her wrist. "Slow down, *Sweetheart*." I bring her wrist down to the mattress, pinning her back, admiring her beauty. Every inch of her is gorgeous.

My lips come down to her neck, pressing a soft trail along her skin, savoring this moment. I don't intend it to only be once, but if I get in my head, I worry that I'll never see her again.

Which is insane.

I can fly out to the nearest landing strip and visit her whenever I feel like it. One of the perks of being a billionaire. My breath tickles her skin as I drop heated kisses before nipping her collarbone. I want to mark her and let every man know that she belongs to me.

Her hips writhe beneath me, grinding and moaning from just my lips alone against her skin. Cali's fingers push at my shirt. Pulling the T-shirt over my head, she helps me undress. Her touch is like lava, hot and flowing through me to my very core.

She tries to roll us around, but I don't let her. "Next time, little one," I whisper, staring down at her with a sly grin. "You need to heal first."

"Little one? I'm not your little anything." She's all bark and no bite. But it's one of the things I love about Cali.

Love.

Inwardly, I grimace, berating myself for using such a word already.

We hardly know each other. But we seem to be getting to know one another really fast.

I growl at her, bringing her bottom lip between my teeth and the moan she elicits sends me into pure bliss. If I died in her arms, I'd be a happy man.

I lift my hips off her body and push my jeans all the way down, kicking them off and to the floor. "You are gorgeous," I whisper, my attention back on her body, worshipping her as I devour every inch of her body.

Pinching the back clasp of her bra, the material slides down with ease, and I lower my lips to her peaks, wanting to watch her squirm under my ministrations.

She shivers and purrs, her legs wrapping around me.

"Still think dinner is better?" I tease, my cheek caressing her stomach, my beard scratchy and thick. I'm gentle over her skin, wanting to excite but not hurt her.

"Deciding," she rasps, but the smile on her face tells me she's as much of a tease as I imagine her to be. She enjoys the attention, and her fingers thread through my hair as my lips move lower.

"How many orgasms have you had in one night?" I ask, climbing down her body and kissing a soft trail up her legs. I start with the backs of her knees, going slow, taking my time, listening to her soft breaths and moans as I inch closer and higher toward her inner thighs.

"With a partner?" she asks, and her fingers claw at the bedsheets. "Or alone?"

I like that she admits to masturbating. Most women shy away from such discussion, which makes me think that next time I might get the pleasure of watching her touch herself for me.

"Partner," I say, my voice betraying me, coming out higher than I intend.

"One."

A wide smirk adorns my face. That will be an easy record to beat. "No one's given you multiple orgasms?" I'm shocked. The woman deserves to feel on top of the world, repeatedly.

"Don't be. I'll be impressed if you can give me one."

"*Sweetheart*, I promise you no less than three."

I swear it feels like a business deal, the way we're bargaining back and forth.

"And if you don't follow through on your commitment?" Cali asks. A sly grin is on her face. Does she have something in mind that she wants from me?

"You don't have to worry about that. By the time we're done, you'll lose count of how many times you scream my name."

I nip her inner thigh playfully, and she moans and tosses her head back, jaw parted, eyes shut. "Look at me," I command.

Her eyes struggle to open, the bluest depths staring back at me. She bites on her bottom lip, and I kiss a trail over her pussy through her panties. I avoid her clit, but run my tongue along her slit, tasting her wetness through the thin fabric.

She wants me to go in for the kill. I can tell she's restless and antsy, but I'm not about to waste her first orgasm without a heavy dose of foreplay. I want her excited, her pussy throbbing, and her begging me to fuck her.

Cali moans, and one hand is roaming through my hair. Her touch feels fantastic. Her other hand twists at the sheets, trembling as I pull her panties to the side and separate her folds, admiring her glistening juices that reveal how turned on she is.

She wiggles her hips.

"Take them off," she says, telling me she wants me to remove her panties. Her fingers land on the elastic band, but I don't follow her instruction.

"Not until you've had your first orgasm," I say.

A whimper spills past her lips, and she covers her face with her hand. "This is torture."

"Do you want me to stop?" I ask.

"No!" Her eyes bolt open, and she glares at me. "I want you to give me an orgasm. One that you rave on about, but I've yet to experience."

She's toying with me, trying to have me give in to her desires.

"And you will, when I'm ready," I say.

With my hand keeping her panties to the side and her pussy exposed, I lick along her slit, tasting her wetness and teasing her swollen lips.

She bends her knees for me. "Good girl," I say as she gives me a better view and more room to lick and suck her pussy. She tastes sweet and sinful. I push my tongue inside her warmth, licking and tongue-fucking her where I want my cock.

Cali shifts her hips, angling her pussy so that I'll reach her clit. "Ask me if I'll touch your clit," I say with a smug smile, and continue tonguing over her wetness and warmth.

"Will you touch my clit?"

"Not yet," I say, teasing her.

She moans and whimpers, and after a few seconds, she brings her hand down between her thighs. I let her touch herself before dragging her fingers into my mouth. I crawl back up her torso, kissing her, tasting her, devouring her lips.

Cali wraps her legs around me, trying to roll us around, but I don't let her. "Logan," she purrs, and it's the first time she's moaned my name tonight. But it won't be the last.

My cock is rock hard. Cali sounds absolutely sinful with my name on her lips. That's not the only thing I want on her lips.

I growl and yank her panties down, ripping the fabric in the process. My cock twitches, and I want desperately to be buried inside of her warmth.

I drag my fingers against her clit, wanting to bring her over the edge, desperate to hear her moans and feel her warmth and tightness surround my shaft.

Her hips gyrate with my hands, and I let her reach her first orgasm, pleased by the gasps and moans that spill from her lips.

Before she has time to recover, I grab a condom and slide it on, teasing her pussy lips with the head of my cock.

"Fuck," she mutters as her body climbs down from her first orgasm.

"We're not done yet, *Sweetheart*." I grab her good leg and lift it to my shoulder, inching my cock inside of her.

She's wet and slick but tighter than I imagined.

"Logan," she moans my name as I push further into her warmth, stretching her and filling her with every inch of me.

Her fingernails trail over my back and down to my ass as she wraps her legs around me.

Her cheeks are flushed, her skin is beautiful and glowing as I fuck her, driving my cock hard and fast inside of her warmth.

She trembles and grips me, securing me like a vice, and her inside walls shudder around me. Pulsating, she moans as the second wave of euphoria hits her.

I keep the pace, not wanting her to lose the orgasm she's chasing as she screams out my name, hands thrashing against the bedsheets before I drag her hands to the bedrail and have her hold on.

Her voice catches in her throat as she shudders around me, tightening onto my cock. "Logan!" she screams, and I swear if anyone is next door at this hour, they can hear us. Hell, most of the floors above and below us can hear her coming.

I want to let go and join her. But I promised her three orgasms, and fuck it, I'm going to deliver on that promise.

Cali gasps for breath, her chest rising and falling as she finally collapses against the mattress, loosening her grip on the headboard rails.

I'd love to have this woman on her hands and knees, but I know that's not possible with the recent bruises from her fall. It's any wonder how she doesn't have a concussion.

"On your side," I command, and guide her onto her side as I get positioned behind her.

"You're not going to do any butt stuff, are you?" she asks, glancing at me over her shoulder.

I chuckle. "It doesn't sound like you're into butt stuff." I'm teasing her, but I wouldn't do anything Cali isn't comfortable with and doesn't consent to.

My fingers graze over her bottom, but my target is her pussy, and I guide my shaft inside her warmth. I let my fingers tease her folds and circle around her clit. But I don't touch the sensitive pearl.

Her back arches, pressing into me as I begin our dance, thrusting and listening to her moaning my name all over again.

"Fuck," Cali grunts, her fingers digging into my hip, roughly caressing me. She's desperate to touch me as I stir another fire deep within her. "I didn't think you could do three," she gasps, trying to catch her breath.

"Oh, I could go all day with you, *Sweetheart*," I say, and mean it. There's something about Cali that makes me alive inside. I can't remember the last time I ever felt this way about anyone.

I can't get enough of her.

Her insides clamp down on my cock, and she's trembling, just barely tinkering on the edge. It's enough to show me she's ready, and I let my fingers press against her clit, teasing and rubbing, as her lips part, and she loudly gasps her enjoyment.

"Cali," I grunt, finding myself closer to the edge. I'm desperately holding on, wanting to ride the last wave in together. I bite down on her shoulder. She moans, clenching on my shaft, her insides spasming as I continue to thrust and tease her clit.

It's actually what she needs, driving her over the edge. Toes curling, gasping and trembling. Her walls clench, refusing to let me go as I bury myself deep within her.

When she releases her grip on me, I climb off the bed and toss the condom in the bathroom trash. My heart pounds wildly against my chest as I'm still catching my breath.

Cali rolls onto her back, her eyelids heavy. "Stay."

I climb into bed beside her, draping an arm over her chest. "For a little bit." I yawn. I can't stay the night. My daughter will worry if I'm not home soon.

But sleep takes hold before I can untangle from her body and pull my clothes on.

Sometime during the night, my phone buzzes, and I groan, realizing I've fallen asleep. I sit up in bed, grabbing my cell phone. It's Julianna.

"Hello?" I rub the sleep from my eyes and try to sound like I've been awake. But it's well past one in the morning.

"Are you okay? You haven't come home," Julianna says.

"I'm just looking after Cali," I say, and grimace.

"Is that code for sex?" my daughter asks, and I swear she's probably making a grossed-out face.

"I was helping change her bandages, and we lost track of time." It's a blatant lie, but maybe my fifteen-year-old will believe it.

"Just remember if I stay out past curfew, it's because I'm changing my friend's bandages."

Nothing gets past this kid. "I'll be upstairs in a few minutes. You need to be in bed. Tomorrow is a workday."

Julianna groans. "Fine. Next time, I won't call to see if you're still alive." She ends the call, and I climb off the bed, retrieving my clothes from the floor.

"Your daughter?" Cali asks, sitting up in bed. She grabs the blankets, covering herself, not that I didn't see everything a couple of hours ago.

"Yeah, she was worried when I didn't come home." I lean in, dropping a kiss to Cali's lips, my fingers curling in her hair, pulling her tighter to me.

She moans and tries to lie back down, bringing me with her.

Reluctantly, I break the kiss apart. "Come find me tomorrow when you're awake. We can get breakfast together."

"That's such a domestic thing," Cali teases. "And I plan on sleeping in. You have to work. I don't."

She pulls the covers up around herself.

"Brunch?" I suggest.

"Maybe." Her eyelids flutter closed, and I'm not sure if she's brushing me off or just that tired. I did wear her out. But it was worth it.

EIGHT

Cali

I CAN'T BELIEVE I had sex with Logan Henderson. My knees are like jelly, and my insides throb just thinking about that man's cock inside of me.

He lived up to his promise of gifting me with three orgasms. And each was more intense than the last.

Tomorrow morning I have to leave early for the airport, so I spend the day lounging around in my pajamas and packing up my belongings. In the afternoon, I take a ride share to the nearest town to get a new cell phone since mine seems to be toast.

It's buried in the snow, but thankfully, even from far away, the phone can be locked if anyone gets ahold of it.

I haven't seen Logan since early this morning when he left and went back to his room. Not that I don't want to see him. I do want to say a proper goodbye, but I'm honestly not sure what he's going to want after last night.

He's not a man interested in a fling, but isn't that what we did? We're not dating. We don't even live in the same state. Geographically, at least we're on the same continent and near the same coast. But that's about it. We live in two very different worlds.

I travel for work, and it's mostly to sunny and warm regions. He lives in the frigid mountains. I'm not sure I could do this year-round. Certainly, if he'd keep my bed warm, it's a possibility, but it was one night together.

The man isn't going to ask me to move in with him and propose.

That would be insane.

There's a firm knock on my bedroom door. "Someone's in here!" I shout. Is it housekeeping?

They haven't come in and made the bed or changed the towels today.

"Cali, open up. It's me." Logan's voice carries through the door.

A small smile tugs at the corners of my lips as I head to the door and pull back the chain, unlocking it. My knee is doing a lot better, along with my ankle. I picked up another elastic bandage, which helps immensely with the pain.

"Hey, come on in." I gesture for him to join me.

"Are you okay? I didn't see you downstairs. Where are your crutches?"

"Probably down in the restaurant still," I say with a laugh. "I'm actually okay. I mean, I should be worse off after that fall yesterday." I almost feel like I'm dreaming and want to wake up. Except the dream is perfect, and I'm afraid to face reality.

"Let me grab the crutches," Logan says, and turns for the door.

"Don't, I'm fine." I show him that I can walk around the hotel room with my boots on. "See, I'm not hobbling."

"Mostly," he admits with a smile. "You do look better. Maybe three orgasms were the medicine you needed to feel better."

I laugh. My cheeks burn just remembering last night. "How is Julianna?" I ask, curious how much of a hard time his daughter gave him when he got home.

"She's downstairs at the equipment rental booth." Logan points at my rental boots. "Do you mind if I take those downstairs?"

"Here on business?" I'm only half-joking. Is that why he came up to my room?

"I wanted to see you. I was hoping we could have brunch, but it's a little late for that now."

The day is half over, but it definitely wasn't wasted. "Sorry, I rushed out earlier today to get a new phone and get everything set up on it. I prefer having my boarding pass on my phone."

Logan nods. "That's right. You're leaving tomorrow." He pauses and stalks closer toward me. "Did you finish your work?"

"My video review?" I shake my head. "I'll splice it together on the plane. I downloaded all the footage from the cloud, so I just have to piece it together the way I want."

"Did you get enough shots? Do you need anything from me?" Logan asks.

I quirk a grin. "I wanted an interview with the owner, but I don't need you to sell this place to the ladies. I'm selfish." I smirk, wanting him to know that he's not going to have all the girls chasing after him when I'm done with the review.

Not that it'll be anything bad, but I don't want the single ladies knowing he's the most eligible billionaire bachelor. I'd sooner call him Mountain Grump than let anyone know the real him.

"I don't think you're selfish," Logan says, wrapping his arms around my waist and pulling me against him. His lips crush mine, and I melt in his arms. "But is it selfish of me if I want you to stay longer?"

I press a kiss to his cheek. "I have to go back home, but we can still be friends."

"I want more than friends with you, Cali. I thought I made that clear."

My breath catches in my throat. "I'd like that too, but I'm not sure how it'll work. I live in Los Angeles, and you live here in Breckenridge."

He presses his lips together and runs his fingers through my hair, dragging my chin up to meet his intense stare. "We can make long-distance work."

I get the feeling he wants more, but it was one night and a week in the mountains.

"Give me your phone," Logan says, and I hand over my new phone, unlocking it. He punches in his phone number and saves it to my contacts. "I expect you to text me when your flight lands and you get home safely."

I don't argue with him, because I know his request is out of concern. He cares about me.

He reaches into his pants pocket and retrieves his cell phone. "Can I get your number?"

I laugh and snatch his phone, punching my digits in while also adding myself as a contact. Instead of putting my name, I type in *My Girlfriend*. I go one step further, giving him my address. Not that I think he'll show up, but I want him to have it.

He shoves his phone into his pocket, not having noticed the name on the contact or my address. It's probably for the best. I don't want him thinking I'm clingy. Because I'm not.

I happen to like Logan, a lot. And I'd love for this to become more than a friends-with-benefits type of situation. Not that we were ever so much as friends. He seemed to hate me when we first met, and well, I wasn't too keen on him, either.

"How about we grab something to eat upstairs? I'd like a do-over for that first night we ate together."

I don't point out that the first night he actually stood his daughter and me up for dinner. Dinner in his place sounds amazing, especially if dessert is involved.

"What about your daughter?" I ask.

"She'll be joining us," Logan says.

I'm not disappointed that I can't have Logan to myself. Instead, it's a strange, warm feeling that seeps into me, making me feel like part of the family. The fact that he wants me around his daughter is a nice change of pace from when we first met.

"Oh, good." I smile and grab a sweater. Not that I expect us to go outside, I'm leaving my coat in the room, but the lodge has some chilly spots.

I leave my phone in my room. The only person I've gotten messages from today was Bridget, wanting an update on my review for the resort. She's anxious to see the video before I post it.

I can't help but wonder what went on between Bridget and Logan. How do they know each other? It was clear he didn't want to discuss it in front of Julianna, but his daughter isn't in my hotel room.

"Can I ask you something?" I shove the room key into my pants pocket, making sure not to lock myself out.

"Anything," Logan says, his eyes staring straight into my soul. I inhale sharply, trying to catch my breath.

"Bridget Lancaster. How well do you know my boss?"

His nostrils flare, and he shoves his hands into his pockets. "She's friends with my ex-wife. Years ago, Bridget hit on me while I was married and didn't seem to care that she and Jess were best friends."

"Some friend she was."

"Oh, I know." Logan's eyes widen. "It gets worse. When Jess was cheating on me, she used to tell me that she was grabbing coffee with Bridget or going to see a chick flick with Bridget. In all honesty, she was using her as an excuse to screw her new fuckboy."

His hands are bunched into fists at his side.

"I'm sorry, I had no idea," I say.

"That woman is the devil."

I don't disagree with him. I've never been particularly fond of Bridget. But there had never been a specific reason not to like her. At times, she was hard on me, but I always took it as her trying to be a mentor to me in the field.

"She's difficult," I say.

"And you work for her." There's a tension that seeps through his veins and makes him stand taller.

"I promise, Logan, I'm nothing like her."

"Good, because I don't deal with liars or cheats." He pulls me into his embrace for a hug. "No more Bridget talk, please?"

I exhale a sigh of relief. The conversation got heavy way too fast. "That works for me."

We head out the door of my hotel room. "Do you need me to carry you?" he asks, sweeping me up off my feet as he brings me down to the elevator.

"I'm fine. Really, you can put me down!" I can't stop laughing until my feet are firmly planted on the ground. Logan keeps his arm around my waist, making sure that I'm steady and won't fall.

He's perfect. Albeit too perfect. Why did his ex-wife ever stray? What crazy woman would break Logan's heart? I never want to be on the other side of his wrath.

"Cali!" Jules' eyes light up when she sees me following Logan inside. "Are you staying for dinner?"

"I am, if that's okay with you." I'm not sure how she's handling the fact that her father is dating. However, she seemed to be shoving us together last night.

"I'd love for you to stay. I mean, for dinner." She clears her throat. "Have you talked to my dad about the summer internship?"

"What's this about an internship?" Logan asks, raising an eyebrow at me.

"Every summer, *Vacationer's Paradise* offers an internship for at least one high school student." Jules' eyes are bright and wide. "I hope it's me!"

"Absolutely not," Logan interjects. "You're not working with Bridget Lancaster."

"But what about Cali? I would work with you, wouldn't I?" Jules asks.

"You would, but your father is right. You'd be directly reporting to Bridget while helping me."

Jules whines and plops down on the sofa in a huff. "That sucks. Why do I get punished for what Bridget and Mom did? How is that fair?"

"Life isn't always fair," Logan says. "The sooner you learn that, the better."

"That's a tough lesson to teach," I say. "I'm sure there are good qualities with Bridget, just like there are good qualities with your mother."

Logan raises an eyebrow. "What are you doing, Cali?"

I honestly don't know. "Trying to soften up some of your grumpiness?"

He steps closer, leaning into my personal space. He's close enough to kiss, but I'm refraining from any sort of intimacy in front of his daughter. I'm not quite sure what's appropriate with her in the room.

"I rather like my level of grumpiness," Logan says.

"I'm with Cali on that one, Dad. You're a super grump."

Logan's cell phone rings, and he glances at the caller before silencing it. "Do you need to take that?" I ask.

"I can call Levi back later. I'm sure it's nothing urgent." Logan drops a soft, chaste kiss on my lips before heading to the fridge. He opens it and retrieves three filet mignons to make for dinner.

"Levi?" I ask, not knowing much about Logan or his friends or family.

"One of my buddies back in New York. He's had a whirlwind of a year. I invited him and the family out to the resort."

"Maybe they'll come visit," Jules says, her eyes brightening. "They have a six-year-old daughter, Amelia. I can't wait to take her down the ski slopes."

Logan glances back at his daughter. "You're not going down those slopes without a parent from now on."

"What?" Jules shrieks. "I didn't fall off the ski lift. How come I'm being punished?"

I bite my tongue. Jules is right, but so is Logan. He just wants what's best for his daughter and I don't want to get in the way. "Can I help with dinner?" I ask, trying to skirt the subject and hopefully change it to something less dramatic.

Jules looks like she may burst into tears at any moment. Her cheeks are red, eyes wide, and she keeps clenching her fists. "It's not fair," Jules whines. "I know how to ski. I've been doing it practically my entire life."

"I know, but I need to get someone on the equipment to make sure the lift isn't faulty. And you know the rules about having a ski buddy. A six-year-old is not an adequate buddy for you."

"Is she any worse than Cali?" Jules asks, and smiles at me. "No offense."

"None taken," I say, although, in truth, it does hurt.

Logan grabs a cutting board from under the counter and begins chopping up garlic and onions. "This discussion is over. We'll worry about it when Levi comes into town with Clare and Amelia. Until then, no skiing without an adult present."

"Cali is an adult and—"

"That's enough!" Logan bellows.

Jules scrunches her nose and huffs under her breath before storming off to her bedroom. She slams the door shut.

"Teenagers," he mutters under his breath.

I stand by the counter, pressing my lips together, wondering what I can do to help. "Do you want me to chop the vegetables?" I offer.

"No, if your cutting skills are anything like your walking skills, you'll leave the sharp knives to me." Logan exhales a heavy sigh. "I'm sorry you had to see that," he says, and gestures toward the back bedroom with Jules.

"It's fine."

"It's not," he says. "She's been a bit moody at times since leaving New York."

"I can't imagine it was easy for her, picking up and leaving everyone she knew behind. But she is making friends. There's Izzie," I remind him. I'd met her friend a few days ago.

"Yeah, Izzie and Julianna go to school together. Those two seem inseparable at times." He's quiet, contemplative, as he cuts the vegetables.

"What is it?" I ask.

"Just thinking about all the different ways I could have you kidnapped and forced to stay at my resort." He chuckles and offers a sly grin. "In all seriousness, I'm going to miss you. In case you couldn't tell."

"You'll miss carrying me to dinner and through the lodge for everyone to watch and wonder what is going on, and when do they get a turn?"

"I'm not carrying anyone else," he says gruffly. "That's reserved just for you."

I rest my hand on my heart. "I'm honored that you'd make me the one and only girl you carry through the resort. Is that something I can get on a plaque?"

"No," he snorts, and shakes his head. "How about you help with the salad? There's a head of lettuce in the fridge. Can you rinse that and just tear it apart. Put it into three bowls."

"Wow, you really don't trust me with a knife." I'm only partially joking. And I don't blame him. I've been clumsy enough this week. Let's not add severed finger to the list of things that went wrong at the resort.

"I don't want us to have to fly to the nearest hospital which is on the other side of the mountain," Logan says.

I open the fridge and retrieve the lettuce, rinsing it in the sink.

"What are your plans for Christmas?" he asks, glancing at me.

If I tell him that I don't do holidays, especially Christmas, he'll think I'm Scrooge. "Nothing special," I say, and force a smile.

"Are you spending it with anyone?" he asks.

"No, I have to get home to finish the video for the vlog and splice it together. Bridget wants it first thing the day after Christmas, so I need to focus, record the voice-over, that sort of thing." I hope he isn't going to ask me to stay for Christmas.

I'm not ready for that level of commitment.

I like Logan, a lot, but he has a daughter, and shouldn't they spend the holiday together, as a family? Besides, his brother is here, and after the spectacle between Wyatt and Logan at the bar, it's better if the three of us don't hang out together.

"That's too bad," he says, his gaze not leaving mine. "I'll have to fly down sometime, visit you when you have time off."

"I'd like that."

A smile grazes his features. "We'll try long-distance ..." His voice trails off, like he's leaving something off, although I'm not sure what.

I let it go, not wanting to push too hard. I've never felt that long-distance relationships last. They may survive for a duration, but not forever. Logan just bought a ski resort and I'm happy in sunny Los Angeles. I don't see us working out in the long run.

The bedroom door squeaks open and Julianna shuffles into the living room. There's a roughness between Logan and his daughter, a tension from the earlier fight that I wish I could let dissipate by opening a window.

I finish with the lettuce and Logan orders his daughter to chop up the other ingredients for the salad. Julianna doesn't argue. Her shoulders are slumped, and she does as he asks without a fuss.

"Dad, do you think maybe we could build a game room on the property?" Julianna asks.

"Do we not have enough video game systems that collect dust around here?" Logan gestures to the living room.

"I mean like arcade-style games. Pacman. Air Hockey. I was asking Izzie if there's an arcade around here for us to go to sometime and she said there isn't any place nearby."

Logan exhales a heavy sigh. "I'll think about it."

"It's a great investment opportunity," Julianna pushes the idea, not backing down. "Teens love to hang out without their parents. It would be a good place in the summer when business is slow for the lodge, or maybe even the evenings. I mean, we don't close for the off-season. The hotel is still open. Why not build an arcade?"

"You'd rather have an arcade over a water slide?"

Julianna's eyes widen, and her lips press together. "You weren't really thinking of turning the pool into an indoor water park. Were you?"

"It crossed my mind. And it would be an expansion, not part of the pool."

"Can we have both?" Julianna asks. "The indoor water park would be great for guests and the arcade is better for locals."

"I'll consider your request," he says. "But I'm not making any promises, about either."

"What do you think?" Julianna asks, staring at me, wanting my input. I'm sure she wants me to side with her and suggest that the arcade and water slide are the way to go for the off-season times.

"I think that's a pretty big investment and a decision that's entirely up to your father."

Logan quirks a grin. "Thanks for staying out of it."

I hold my arms up in surrender. "I won't be here to enjoy the amenities of either."

He groans. "Just what I need, you to drown on a water slide."

Our time spent together feels too short, too fleeting. In the blink of an eye, I'm heading back to the airport, flying home, back to Los Angeles.

The sun is warm, the sky bright, and there's no snow here in December. It's perfect. Except it's missing one thing, well, technically two things. Logan and his daughter.

I spend the holiday making three different video reviews for Blue Sky Resort. All of them praise the amenities that they have to offer. Bridget can decide to use one or all three if she's so inclined. She's always praised me for giving her options, so I save the files when I'm done and load them to the cloud.

Ordinarily, I'd shoot off an email to her, but it's Christmas day, and that seems tacky. Just because I don't have a life, doesn't mean other people aren't busy.

Besides, Bridget doesn't need to know that I'm spending my holiday working. It's not like I'll get a bonus or extra pay. I'm a contractor. There's no salary. No benefits. Sometimes it's grueling. But getting to stay at hotels, living lavishly, and eating and vacationing for free has been a dream come true.

And it's not on my dime, which makes it even better.

I text Logan *Merry Christmas*. Not that I expect to hear back from him. He's busy with his family, as he should be.

My phone pings with a notification. I shouldn't feel quite so giddy about getting a text from him. He's not my boyfriend. I'm honestly not sure what we are, or aren't, for that matter.

What are you up to?

His text brings a smile to my face. The grumpy single dad seems to have turned a corner. Maybe he's not quite so difficult after all.

Just curled up on the sofa with a tub of Ben & Jerry's.

You should have stayed here for Christmas. I could have flown you back first thing in the morning.

A heavy sigh escapes my lips. *I had to get my work done this weekend. Which, I might add, is amazing. You'll be so surprised by what I did that it'll leave you speechless.*

Good or bad?

You'll have to wait and see, I text, hoping he knows it's good. I just like keeping the man on his toes.

If it's bad, I'd hope you'd tell me what went wrong, and I could rectify it for other guests.

Is he worried I'll give him a one-star review and blast the resort? I put my ice cream container down on the coffee table while I text him back.

Do you mean falling from the ski lift and nearly dying wasn't cause enough?

I'm joking with him. At least, I think he should know that much about me by now. We've spent enough time knocking heads and a few times, boots, to get past the bad stuff that happened.

He begins typing. Three dots flash while he's answering before disappearing.

Silence.

It's Christmas Day. He's probably busy and got pulled away from his phone by Julianna or Wyatt.

That's all it is, right? I was joking. He had to know that I'd never write or say a bad thing about him or his resort.

When the vlog is posted, he'll see that I gave him five stars and a rave review.

The next day at work, I'm at my desk in my office, piecing together one last clip. Not that Bridget needs a fourth, but I want something fun that showcases Logan. I took a few clips, zooming in on his thick, bulging arms tattered in ink. An angry and fierce shot of him storming away, his hands are balled into fists at his side.

A shiver runs down my spine.

Even when he's steaming, he's hot.

Bridget's heels clank over the floor as she heads to my office. I glance up from my monitor as she enters without so much as a greeting. "I reviewed your videos." There's no smile on her face, no glint in her eyes of a job well done.

She comes to my desk, sitting across from me in the vacant chair. "I've put you on a lot of assignments, Cali. I've trusted you to give an honest portrayal of a resort. I can't understand how you can give the place where you sprained your ankle and fell out of a ski lift a five-star review."

"Those things weren't his—the Blue Sky Resort's fault."

Her eyes tighten, and her jaw grinds as she clenches her teeth. "The fact that you fell out of a ski lift proves the place is dangerous. Had the equipment malfunctioned, or was there no bar to keep you in place? Either way, it's a lawsuit waiting to happen. I'll reach out to a lawyer, and we can sue for damages."

"There weren't any—" I begin, and Bridget cuts me off.

"I know you like to see everything with a cheery and sunny disposition. I thought that sending you to the mountains, in a cold, wintery climate, would help give you a little perspective when creating your next video. Our viewers don't want to see five stars for every destination we review."

"I don't always give five stars. I gave that Jamaican resort with the dirty linens four stars."

Bridget rolls her eyes, unimpressed. "You're not brutal enough. I sent you to the mountains expecting a one-star review. You hate the cold, you've never gone skiing in your life, and it's the middle of winter. It's too bad there wasn't a blizzard, and you got snowed into the resort. You could have seen how little there was to do outside of skiing."

"It's a ski resort," I say. "I wasn't expecting a day spa and a beach."

Bridget stands, miffed at my rebuttal. "I don't need your attitude, and frankly, I'm not paying you to go on vacation and leave boring five-star reviews. We need to be edgy and innovative. We want to be a leader in the leisure category. That's not going to happen with you on our platform."

My head spins, and my mouth drops. "Are you firing me?"

"I'm letting you go," Bridget says. "The video footage that you're working on is our property. You're not to touch any of it or post it anywhere. Is that understood? We paid for your trip. The footage that you shot belongs to us."

I exhale a heavy sigh. "Yes, I know the terms under my contract."

"Good. Pack your desk. I want you out immediately."

NINE

Logan

I HAVEN'T HEARD from Cali. Not so much as a good morning text or a note that I should check for her video review.

My stomach keeps grumbling, and I shut it up with more coffee. I'm jittery, and the caffeine doesn't help.

Cali enjoyed her time immensely at the resort, but was it because of me or because the resort deserves a high star rating?

I believe we're worthy of five stars, but does she think the same? She did fall off the ski lift, which, according to Julianna, had nothing to do with a malfunction and everything to do with Cali being careless.

The girl should be surrounded by bubble wrap.

I glance at my phone. Should I text her? She was the last one to respond, and I never answered her back.

I stalk the clock app where Cali posts her video reviews for Vacationer's Paradise. A new video was posted two minutes ago.

Exhaling a sigh, I click on the video, and every fear inside of me is nothing compared to the horror I witness. There's a close-up of my biceps, the tattoos that cover my arms. I'm not as tan as I'd like, but it's December.

There's no voice-over, just captions that pop up throughout the video.

Billionaire Logan Henderson, owner of Blue Sky Resort.

Okay, so the video review focuses a little too much on me, but maybe that's my fault. I did sleep with Cali.

Easy on the eyes. Awful on the slopes.

There's footage of a ski lessons group learning to take the bunny hills, quite a few of them falling and tumbling into each other.

But it's not me on the slopes. Is she insinuating that I don't know how to ski? Cali never saw me on skis. I rub the back of my neck and watch in horror as the video goes from bad to worse.

Dodgy. Dangerous. Deadly. Would you let your kid ski here?

It's an attack ad, worse than the mudslinging that goes on during an election campaign.

The video shows Julianna and her friend Izzie snowboarding down the slopes. They're doing everything that I've taught my daughter, including wearing a helmet for protection. But Izzie wipes out in the snow.

And then the real nightmare begins. There's raw footage from the security feeds of Cali slipping out of the ski lift and falling. We don't see it only once. It's replayed in slow motion three times over.

Is she trying to wreck the ski lodge? Does she want me to go out of business and close the resort? Because the video is pretty damning.

Billionaire Logan Henderson should stick to what he knows. The big city.

I should shut off the video. It's obvious that nothing good will come of anyone seeing it. The saying about there's no such thing as bad press never met Cali Sinclair.

The woman is brutal.

Vicious.

A true savage.

The only thing I regret more than helping her while she was here is sleeping with her.

I can't watch the rest of the video. I swipe the app and close it, shoving my chair out from under my desk. Work has to wait. I want every reminder of Cali removed from my home and the lodge.

While I can't burn memories, I can destroy the things that she touched. My bed sheets, for starters. The last night together when she stayed over after Julianna went to bed.

The first thing on the list to be destroyed is the white linens.

I never want to smell her scent again. Her pheromones are addictive and hypnotic. The woman, like a witch, lured me into bed with her, pretending to be someone she's not.

I head straight for the elevator when Julianna rounds the corner. "Dad!" she calls, chasing after me.

I hit the button for the elevator. I don't want to talk to anyone.

But Julianna runs faster and slides between the double doors as they're closing. "Dammit, Julianna!" I shout. She could have gotten hurt with her aggressive maneuver.

I slide the key into the lock for the penthouse suite and hit the button.

"I guess you saw the vlog this morning," Julianna says. She tugs her bottom lip between her teeth. Her eyes glisten with tears.

I wrap my arm around her shoulder. "I'm sorry." I shake my head, angry with myself for trusting that little witch. "I should have known not to trust her. She's practically media, and they always distort the truth." I've seen it countless times, not necessarily with myself but with others I know.

"It's not your fault that she betrayed us. And she made Izzie look like a fool!" Julianna's bottom lip trembles. "If Izzie sees the video of her wiping out, she'll never forgive me."

I clear my throat and stand up straighter. "I'll reach out to my lawyer and have the footage removed."

"Dad, no!" Julianna's eyes widen. "That will only make it worse. Just leave it alone. Don't draw any more attention to the review. Maybe it'll go away."

It won't disappear on its own, but I appreciate my daughter's sentiment. We reach the top floor, and the double doors open.

Julianna steps out first, and I head straight for the bedroom. I'm not sure Julianna is aware that Cali slept over. We tried keeping it a secret.

I yank the covers and sheets from the bed. The room smells like Cali, with hints of almond, vanilla, and lavender. It tickles my nose, burning my senses. I want all of it destroyed.

My daughter opens her mouth to say something but quickly shuts it. "Have you tried calling Cali?"

"Why would I?" She made it clear with the review that she was only interested in destroying me. The woman didn't give a damn about my feelings, or my daughter's, for that matter.

Julianna doesn't answer. She shakes her head and opens the double door to the balcony, letting fresh air into the bedroom.

Anything to remove the aroma of Cali on my sheets. It's intoxicating.

We strip the bed, and while I'd like to burn the sheets physically, Julianna talks me into having our housekeeping service wash them and replace them with new linens. We can always donate the old bed sheets. They're still in impeccable shape. Practically new.

My phone rings, and I dig into my pocket, unsure if it's Wyatt needing help downstairs or someone else looking for me to answer a question or help with a guest.

I glance at the caller ID and reject the call.

"Cali?" Julianna asks, glancing over my shoulder as I block her number.

I never want to speak with her again.

Some betrayals cut deep and destroy a person from the inside out. I have enough trouble with learning to trust another person after my ex cheated on me with my best friend.

What Cali did, the pain burns just as bright, searing and forcing me to bleed out emotionally. I never expected her deception. Maybe I should have realized that women can't be trusted after my wife played me.

I didn't expect betrayal from Cali. I never expected the brunette to have a dark side. She'd always been sunny, carefree, and sweet. Was it all an act?

She had me fooled.

"You're not going to answer her call?" Julianna asks.

"There's no reason. She just wanted to make a viral video. Let's just hope it doesn't work." I hand my daughter my cell phone. "Delete that clock app from my phone. I never want to see it or any of her videos again."

"You can just block her on the app," Julianna says.

I raise an eyebrow. "Delete it." She's lucky I'm not making her delete the app from her phone too. "Let this be a lesson, young lady. Influencers chase after the next big trend. They're in it for the views and likes. They don't care who they hurt or destroy in the process."

"That's not always true," Julianna says. She taps at my phone, deleting the app, before handing me back the device. "I'm bummed that I won't be interning for Cali this summer."

I can't have this conversation with Julianna. If it were up to me, I'd keep her away from all influencers and social media. It's not healthy for her, trailing after someone who wants to be famous and watch them destroy another person's life.

I storm out of the bedroom, leaving the sheets in a bunch on the floor. I stomp into the living room. Two throw pillows remind me of Cali, even though they were there long before she stepped foot in the penthouse. She'd nestled her head on one pillow while it was in my lap, and the other she'd held tight against her chest.

I grab the throw pillows and toss them into the bedroom on the floor with the pile of sheets and blankets.

"Call housekeeping and have them remove the linens and pillows on the floor. I never want to see that stuff again."

———

I do everything I can to forget about Cali. To purge her from my memory. Her scent. Her touch. The taste of her on my lips.

For the next few days, I drown myself in liquor until Wyatt steals the bottles from the penthouse, and I'm too tired to wander down to the bar.

If Cali tries to call, I don't know about it. Her number is blocked. I contemplate unblocking, but the urge passes as quickly as it came.

I despise her.

That woman knew how to destroy me faster than anyone I've ever met. It's disgusting. Repulsive. Vile.

My eyes burn, but I don't cry. I'm not a man who sheds tears over a woman I hardly knew.

"Are you going to lock yourself in here forever?" Wyatt asks. He folds his arms across his chest.

"Seems like the thing to do. She's destroyed my business."

"No, you're doing that, moping around the penthouse instead of greeting guests and helping staff. You know this time of year is busy for the resort."

"We had a bunch of cancellations." I blame it on Cali and her attempt to destroy us.

"That's because the airlines have been overbooked. Some are on strike. You can't blame Cali for guests being unable to show up. And that doesn't include the weather causing cancellations either. It's December. Snowstorms happen."

"Those are excuses. After New Year's, you'll see things don't start picking back up."

"Well, the kids will be back in school," Wyatt says. "Try to relax. Get a massage or something. Find a cute little blonde at the bar. Bang it out and move the fuck on."

I groan and run a hand through my hair. "I don't bang anything out."

"And that's your problem," Wyatt says.

"No," I growl. "My problem is that I slept with Cali and trusted her. And you see where that got me?"

Wyatt shrugs. "Not all women are witches. You just have bad luck. Maybe let me meet them before you sleep with them."

I glare at my younger brother. "Did you forget meeting Cali?"

A wry grin spreads across his face. He certainly didn't warn me she could be trouble. But I should have seen that from a mile away. All the red flags flying in the wind. From the moment I met her, the woman was out for blood.

First, it was the prices she thought were outrageous.

"I've got a surprise for you," Wyatt says.

I've had enough surprises for a lifetime. "No thanks." I sip my beer. It's all that's left in the penthouse in terms of alcohol. Wyatt doesn't think I can get trashed on beer. Well, I can certainly try.

"You'll like this surprise. Just stay put. Don't do anything stupid."

I glare at him as he heads toward the elevator. I swear if he brings Cali up, I'll kill him. And then I'll have a screaming match with her until my lungs no longer have air in them to breathe.

I guzzle the beer and grab a second one, wishing I could have something a little harder with more bite.

A few minutes later, Wyatt is coming back up to the room. This time, he brought my old friend, Levi Luxenberg, from New York.

"Levi," I say, staring at the elevator, glassy-eyed. I'm relieved it's not Cali and disappointed at the same time.

What the hell is wrong with me?

"Logan," Levi says, and steps into the penthouse. Whether I invite him in or not, he's making himself at home. He heads straight for the fridge and grabs a beer for himself. "You want one?" he asks my brother.

"I'm good," Wyatt says, and shakes his head.

"Why? It's not like you need to be sober. You're not going anywhere tonight," I mutter.

Both men choose to ignore my remark. I glance at Levi. "Where's Amelia?" I ask.

I commend him for it. Most guys would have let the kid rot in foster care.

Levi isn't most guys.

"She's with Clare downstairs, grabbing a bite to eat. They found Julianna and are catching up."

I groan. The thought of Levi bringing his new love hurts. It shouldn't. I should be happy for the two of them.

I want to be happy for him, but I'm wallowing in my self-made misery.

"Long flight?" I ask, taking another swig of my beer, trying desperately to talk about anything but his love life. I'm happy he met someone, but I'm in more of a feral mood than anything else.

It's good Amelia and the girlfriend didn't come up to the penthouse. I wouldn't be a very good host.

"Not too bad," Levi says.

He always flies private. Well, almost always. He has a great story about the one time he flew commercial and how he met the nanny for his daughter. Usually, it's sweet and a story I like hearing, but right now, it's too syrupy.

"Wyatt told me about the influencer," Levi says.

"He did?" I glare at my brother. "Did he happen to show you the video she made, too?"

Levi clears his throat. His brow is tight, and I can't tell if he's seen the video because Wyatt sent it to him or because it's viral, and he feels sorry for me.

I don't want to know. I'd rather be like a turtle and bury myself inside my shell. Become a recluse. Not have to converse with anyone.

"I saw it," Levi says. "But I wouldn't worry about it. She wasn't to be trusted. You'll meet another girl who doesn't intend on murdering you in your sleep."

I think he's joking, but I don't smile. Levi, however, is grinning. "Relax. I came here to offer a few ideas."

"Ideas?" He's done well turning the hotel chain that he owns around. He inherited the business from his father, but it was struggling when he took control.

"For starters, maybe what the girl did was wrong, but the idea behind it was good."

I'm not following, and there's not even a hint of a smile on my face. I'm exhausted. I don't feel like talking about shop at this hour. "Can we leave the business discussion for tomorrow?" I ask.

I tilt my head back and crack my neck from side to side before taking the last swig of my beer. I grab another from the fridge and gesture for him to join me on the sofa. It's not like he's leaving anytime soon.

Levi had talked about coming for a few days, bringing Amelia, to give her snowboard lessons. I just hadn't expected them to show up unannounced and uninvited. Although, I get the feeling Wyatt invited them to stay.

And it's not like we don't have room at the resort.

"Yeah, sure," Levi says. "Whatever you want."

I want to forget about the gorgeous brunette with blue eyes and a sexy ass. I want to purge her from my mind, and if I could have a do-over, I'd change everything about how we met. I wouldn't have carried her to dinner or paid her the least bit of attention.

When she was injured, I'd have had another staff member rescue her, and I certainly wouldn't have climbed into her bed and given her three orgasms.

My hands bunch into fists.

I would never have let her into my penthouse. Cooked her dinner. Let her become part of my family with my daughter, sharing a meal and then sneaking her into my bedroom after a movie in the living room.

I've never regretted something or someone so much in my life.

I'm the only one to blame.

Trusting her was my fault. I knew after Jess that I should never trust another woman, minus my daughter, and I went head-first into fucking Cali because my cock had a mind of its own.

Never again.

TEN

Cali

THERE ARE no unemployment benefits when you're axed from a contractor position. So, I'm stuck looking for a job anywhere.

The Los Angeles job market seems pretty tight. Everyone wants to either underpay for the position or hire an intern. Neither of those work for me.

And I need something full-time.

Looking back, I had an office and set hours. I'm pretty sure Bridget should have been paying me as an employee and not as a contractor. She was trying to get away with not having to pay benefits, including social security tax, which I got stuck footing.

Could I get her into trouble for it? Yes, but it's not worth the hassle.

That woman screwed me over.

I just want to move on and never look back.

She took the footage I had, changed it, manipulated it, and then posted it online, making Logan out to be the bad guy, which is completely untrue and unfair.

While he was a bit of a grump when I first got to know him, the captions she put on the video were entirely unfair.

I watched it once and grimaced. I couldn't watch it again and didn't want to give her any extra video views by repeatedly watching it, either.

I tried calling Logan. He wouldn't take my calls. I don't have Julianna's number or Wyatt's. When I tried to call the hotel and get transferred, Wyatt told me to leave Logan alone and hung up abruptly.

No one would let me explain what happened.

If I had the money, I'd fly to Breckenridge and explain everything to Logan. But I don't have the funds. I can barely make ends meet since my last paycheck was short. Bridget decided not to pay me for my services for the last assignment, since she didn't use the footage I put together.

Except, she did use it. She spliced up the clips I had and made it into her own horror story, giving the resort zero stars. That's not even something we do!

Did Bridget have it out for Logan from the beginning?

Obviously, there's bad blood between the two of them. And she made it clear that she expected me to create a scathing video review. It's why she sent me to the mountains when she knows I hate the cold.

That woman is vile.

But Logan thinks I'm the monster who sold him out. It wasn't me, and if he won't take my calls, how am I supposed to explain to him what happened?

I wrote him a letter, but it came back as refused. He didn't even open it.

He hates me.

There isn't anything to do but move on. Find another job and chalk this up as a history lesson. Don't mix business and pleasure.

I shouldn't have slept with Logan. Not that I regret a moment of it, but it wasn't a wise decision.

It's been weeks since I've seen him or spoken with him. I have an interview lined up out of state. I can't afford the plane fare, but the company has offered to fly me out after doing two phone and video interviews with staff.

They're looking to expand their hotel line in several overseas markets. They want an influencer who can help push them on social media, encouraging travel to those countries and thinking of the Luxenberg line of hotels to stay at.

I don't complain. It's a job, and the pay has to be better than what I was making. Besides, I'm late on my bills and put everything on my credit card so that I can make rent.

I can't keep doing that. I need a job, even if it's flipping burgers or making sandwiches. That's my next option if this doesn't pan out.

I haven't been to New York before. It's winter, February, and chilly. There's snow on the ground but not too much to cause me to be late for the interview. But I'm not dressed warm enough for the cold.

I'm shivering as I rush into the building, my black heels sliding out from under me on the icy pavement.

I curse, but manage to catch myself before landing on my ass or skinning my knee. I don't need torn pantyhose as a first impression.

My neck is sore, and my arm hurts from trying to catch myself. I managed to pull a muscle, but it could be worse.

I hate heels. I'm only wearing them to look the part of a professional. I've met with several staff members via video conference, but they're having me meet the CEO in person.

I check in at the main desk and am handed a visitor pass and pointed toward the direction of the elevators.

I head into the elevator, exhaling a heavy sigh. As instructed, I press the button for the thirty-fifth floor, and the elevator car zooms up at record speed. My heart pounds in my chest, and my stomach is a ball of nerves. I barely touched my breakfast this morning, afraid I'd get sick.

I shouldn't be nervous, but this is a big company and a huge interview. If I get the job, I'll probably have to move to New York, but at least I'll be able to pay my bills.

Not that New York City is cheaper than Los Angeles.

I should have looked for a job in some small town with a company requiring a social media presence. Except a small town is what led me to Logan Henderson, and I don't want to go down that path again.

Small towns mean that everyone knows one another. There are no secrets. If you date someone and it doesn't work out, you'll always see them at the grocery store, gas station, or restaurant. No thanks.

I'm done with that life. One week was too much.

The elevator doors ding as I reach the thirty-fifth floor and step out. There's another reception desk at the front.

"May I help you?"

"Yes, I'm here to see Mr. Luxenberg. I have an appointment with him."

"And you are?" the woman asks.

"Cali Sinclair."

"Just a second," she says, and grabs the phone, letting him know that his interviewee has arrived.

"Head on in. It's straight back and down the hallway." The woman gestures for me to go on ahead. And while I'm surprised no one is walking me back, it's clear that everyone is incredibly busy.

The door is shut, and as I approach, it swings open. Logan steps out. "Cali?"

"Logan?" I say, staring up at him. It's like having the wind knocked right out of me. "I—" I have so much to say, but it doesn't come out as quickly as I'd like.

"Ms. Sinclair?" a gentleman's voice booms from the office, waiting for me to enter.

"I have to go," I say, pointing at the door. "I'm sorry about everything." I chew on my bottom lip, making it raw as I slip past Logan and shut the door. I'm unsure if Mr. Luxenberg wants the office door shut, but I don't want Logan hanging around.

In fact, how do Logan and Mr. Luxenberg know one another?

The gentleman behind the desk stands and approaches me, shaking my hand. "I'm Levi, and you must be Ms. Sinclair."

"Please, call me Cali," I say. If he's not going to be formal, neither will I.

"Please, have a seat," Levi says.

I do as he requests, sitting across from him while he glances over my resume. His eyes crinkle, and he offers a tight-lipped smile. "What brings you all the way from California, and don't just tell me it's the job."

I exhale a heavy breath.

Shit.

If Levi and Logan are friends, he'll never hire me if he discovers who I am.

"Long story," I say, and wave my hand dismissively. "It's not very interesting. I'm looking for a fresh start."

The office door squeaks open, and Logan returns with a hot cup of coffee.

My day just went from bad to worse.

"Mr. Henderson will join us for the interview," Levi says. "We're looking to expand our social media to our ski resort."

"What?" My head swims. "In the previous interview, the woman, Janet, had mentioned that you were looking for someone to do social media campaigns for Europe."

"We were, but that position has been filled internally. The job description remains the same. You would just be working on a different product line. Is that a problem?" Levi asks.

I inhale a sharp breath. "Of course not," I say, forcing a smile.

Logan sips his coffee, standing by the door.

"Are you going to sit?" Levi asks, glancing at his colleague.

I hadn't realized that Logan was involved with Luxenberg Enterprises. Had he sold his ski resort to a big corporation after the terrible video review Bridget created and posted online?

Logan comes around and leans against the wall between Levi and me. "I'd like to hear about your previous experience. A recent campaign that you did that had a negative impact."

He can't be serious.

Now is my chance to apologize and right everything that went wrong. But will he accept my apology?

I need this job to pay my bills. I can't keep pushing off my credit card, adding my bills and rent to it, and paying the minimum.

I fidget in my seat, straighten my back and make sure my feet are planted firmly on the floor. "I never created a campaign that had a negative impact."

"We don't hire liars," Logan says, pushing himself off the wall, standing up straighter.

"There have been some campaigns that I've done that weren't as successful as others, but I've never willfully hurt a company or their reputation."

"Bullshit."

Levi raises an eyebrow. "I take it you two know each other?" He leans back in his chair, folding his arms across his chest.

The man will get a show, whether he wants one or not.

"She's the girl who posted that video review that tried to destroy my company. There's no way in hell I'm hiring her to work for me," Logan says.

"Can I explain?"

"Please do," Levi says. He glances at my resume and grabs a pen from his desk, jotting something down.

"I'm not sticking around to hear your excuses." Logan heads for the door.

"I'm sorry," I say. "But it wasn't my video review. Bridget took my footage and made her own creative to post."

Logan pauses at the door and huffs under his breath. "Nice try." He opens the door and heads out, refusing to look at me.

Levi grimaces and folds his hands together. "Unfortunately, even if you are the right candidate, you would have to work directly under Logan Henderson, full-time. I don't suspect that's possible."

I grimace and shake my head. "I didn't come here to work for Logan." Not that he'd hire me, either. "But I would like to explain what happened." While I doubt Levi will side with me or talk to Logan about it, maybe he can find another opportunity within his company for me. Another branch to work out of?

"I saw the video. I should have put two and two together. It didn't cross my mind that you might be the same Cali Sinclair as the girl back in California who trampled on my friend's heart."

I wince. "The video you saw wasn't what I created." I shove my hand into my pocket, retrieving a flash drive. "I have several video reviews along with other samples that I've curated for this interview." I slide the small device across the desk. "Please, take it."

"Can you explain why you left your previous position?" Levi asks.

"My boss, Bridget Lancaster, insisted that I stop giving positive five-star reviews to resorts I visit. She sent me to the mountains in winter, hoping I'd get her hint and create a scathing piece for the vlog."

"And what happened?"

I point at the flash drive. "You can view the creatives I made for the Blue Sky Resort. They showcase what I'm capable of doing, and I assure you that while the video footage you might have seen from Vacationer's Paradise was mine, not all of it was intended to be shown. And the captions and audio were not my work."

Levi offers me a warm smile. "I will review these and look further at your portfolio. But you should know that Logan will be the one making the final decision."

"May I ask how many other candidates you have narrowed down for the job?" They flew me from California. I should have had a pretty good chance of landing the position before Logan showed up.

But it's not his fault. I hadn't been told I would be working on a resort project in the mountains.

"There are a few candidates," Levi says, tightlipped. "While the original job listing would have required the candidate to relocate to New York, this position would require you to live in Montana."

I laugh under my breath.

"Is that a problem, Ms. Sinclair?" Levi asks.

"No, sir. But if I'm to be frank, I don't think Logan will ever approve of it, and I can't imagine we would work well together."

Levi nods and jots something down. "Let me talk it over with him. We will be in touch." He stands and escorts me out of his office, down the hallway, past Logan, who is stewing with the receptionist near the elevator.

She's probably getting an earful.

Is he sleeping with her, too?

ELEVEN

Logan

"YOU COULD HAVE WARNED ME!" My body tingles with rage, like a volcano ready to burst at any moment.

A few staff members are looking in our direction in the hallway.

Cali is in the elevator on her way down. I wait as patiently as possible before my sudden outburst.

"Let's discuss this in private," Levi says, and heads for his office.

I'm not one of his staff members. I don't work for Levi Luxenberg. We're equals. Well, technically, I'm the bigger shareholder in the resort.

When he came to visit in December, he shot off a few decent ideas that made me consider making him part owner. He receives a small percentage in addition to a royalty share for every slope ticket that we sell for the day.

In exchange, he'll be doing the official hiring of our social media expert, who is going to help our image and give us the publicity we need. The position works under my leadership but is paid through Luxenberg Enterprises. The employee will report to me and be required to live in or near Breckenridge. It's not a position that can be done from home or across the country.

He shuts the office door more gently than I would as I storm inside. "Do you think this is funny, bringing Cali here for an interview?" I want to pound the shit out of something or someone. Maybe I should find the fitness room. Levi is bound to have one in the building for his employees.

Levi smiles, his shoulders relaxed. He's not the least bit tense or high-strung over what just happened. It must be nice.

"I was as surprised as you were," he says. He comes to sit behind his desk and grabs the flash drive off his desk, plugging it into the slot. "But you did say the video she made got a lot of traffic."

"Wyatt told me that. I haven't looked at it since the day after Christmas." It's ingrained in my mind, the horrible things she said about the company and me. It's hard to separate the two when I own the establishment and live there. I take pride in my work and my accomplishments.

I should be grateful I haven't seen anything from a lawyer after Cali fell from the ski lift.

"Did you know that Cali used to work for Bridget Lancaster?" Levi asks.

I rub the back of my neck and sit in the chair across from Levi. "She mentioned it a while back." I forgot. It was an easy thing to axe out of my mind after everything else that happened.

"That woman always had it out for you."

"Every woman seems to have it out for me," I mutter. Cali included.

Levi chooses to ignore my remark. I'm sure he realizes nothing good will come from fighting with me about it. "Cali sent me a few additional samples. She claims that the video we saw on the vlog wasn't hers."

"Who else shot the footage?"

"She's not saying she didn't shoot it, but the review and the captions weren't her. She left her job that morning, or was fired," he says.

"I don't understand."

"I believe Bridget made the video and, in the same process, let Cali go because she didn't do what she wanted her to do."

I laugh under my breath. "So, Cali isn't a model employee."

Levi opens the folder on the computer with the flash drive and turns the screen so we can both view the content. He goes through the first video, which showcases Blue Sky Resort, and the video footage is on the slopes, with kids and families laughing and having a good time. There's a video of the lodge, the restaurant, the food at the table, and the shop. The review is positive and upbeat.

I stand, having seen enough. "She must have known she was coming in for an interview for my resort."

"I don't think that's possible. The job listing didn't mention it, and it wasn't until yesterday that we officially made the internal transfer for another position, or else you would have had another candidate for the job."

I don't know who the other candidate is, but it has to be better than dealing with Cali every damn day. "I want the other candidate," I say.

"That's not an option. We mentioned to her that the position would require her to move to Montana, and she refused. She asked if she could switch to the new division for our international social media projects. Given her experience and years with the company, it was the best decision for everyone."

"Everyone but me."

"I found you a spectacular candidate. I can't help that the two of you hate each other."

I open my mouth to object and tell Levi I don't hate her, except I can't. I'm angry. Bitter. Resentful.

"Why did she really leave *Vacationer's Paradise*?" I ask.

"You'll have to ask her that question," Levi says. He starts the next video clip, and it's similar to the last, the text is different, but it's another five-star raving review. "But it's clear in the creative content that the video on their website, she didn't create. She may have filmed the clips, but that's all she's responsible for doing. The text is different, the design layout."

"How the hell did they get surveillance footage of her fall?" I ask, remembering the original had a clip of her falling from the ski lift, which was shown repeatedly.

"A lawyer didn't reach out to you?" Levi asks. "I assumed someone requested the footage as part of an ongoing lawsuit."

"Nothing."

He exhales a heavy breath and strokes his jaw. "That's odd and interesting at the same time. I don't think Cali is behind it. She doesn't seem the type."

"She tried to destroy my company with a single video. What makes you think that she's not the type?" I growl.

Levi stands and approaches a mini fridge in his office. He opens it and grabs two bottles of water.

"I'm not thirsty," I say.

He shoves the bottle into my hands. "You've had enough caffeine, and it's too early to be drinking anything available at a bar. Water," he says, like it's a command.

Damn him.

I unscrew the lid and take a swig. "That woman irritates me, Levi. I can't work with her."

"She's quite talented." He ignores me and plays the third video clip from the file. There are more graphics, text, and a voiceover featuring Cali.

I suck in a breath, and my fingers involuntarily crunch the open bottle of water in my hand, splashing myself. I curse and jump up, removing my suit coat. "Any chance you have paper towels lying around?"

"There's a hand dryer in the bathroom."

I grumble and stalk out of his office, my shirt soaked. I get a few strange looks on my way in, but thankfully the water didn't land on my crotch. That's the only thing that could have made this day worse.

After work, Levi and I head to the bar to blow off some steam. Amelia is with Clare.

"How are you and Clare doing?" I ask, wanting to talk about anything other than Cali and the interviews. We had two interviews, including Cali's, and it was clear that she was the girl for the job. But I'm convinced anyone else would still be better than butting heads with the beautiful vixen who stole my heart and stomped on it publicly for everyone to see.

At least, that's how it feels.

I'm a tad overdramatic, but I can't help that I'm angry with her, and the only way to erase that pain is with a few drinks. At least it'll dull it.

"Clare is good. We're both taking things slow," Levi says.

"Slow? You're fucking the nanny."

"Don't be so crass. I love the woman, and she's great with Amelia. The fact that she happens to be the nanny is an added perk. And, not that we're telling anyone, but we're trying for a boy."

"Is that a thing?" I ask, sipping my bourbon. "Like special positions or some shit to make sure it's a boy instead of a girl?" Jess and I only ever had one child, Julianna, who wasn't the least bit planned. Jess never wanted any more kids.

"That would be fun," Levi says with a wicked grin, "but I don't think that's how it works. Maybe, though, we'll try it. Google it on the internet."

I finish my bourbon and order another. I'm within walking distance to the hotel where I'm staying at one of Levi's properties. I don't have to worry about getting behind the wheel of a car or even walking far.

"How is Jules doing? Is Wyatt watching her while you're here?"

"Yeah," I say, and glance at my phone. "I called and left her a message, but she was spending the night over Izzie's." My jaw tightens.

"You look stressed."

"When am I not stressed? I can't tell if Julianna's sleepover is just girls hanging out type of thing or something more. And if it's something more, I feel like, at fifteen, she should not be spending the night."

"What do you mean?" Levi asks.

"Julianna likes girls." I had less issue with it when they were sleeping under my roof and I was the parent who was home.

"Well, she can't get pregnant." Levi slaps my back. "Relax. She's a teenager. They explore and whatnot. Remember when we were that age? Let's not think about that tonight, okay?"

I groan. Easier said than done. "Just wait until Amelia is fifteen and old enough to date."

Levi's top lip snarls. "Shut your mouth. My daughter isn't dating anyone until she's thirty."

"Good luck keeping her from breaking that crazy rule." Although it doesn't sound half-bad. If I could keep Julianna from dating anyone until she was thirty—male or female—I'd be all for it.

I consume more alcohol than I should in a few short hours. Women are dancing, and a few come up to me, asking for a dance, wanting me to take them home.

I'm not interested.

They're pale compared to the brightness of Cali. The woman crept not only into my heart and thoughts, but into the city. Why can't she stay on the west coast? Why did she have to apply for a job and come to New York?

Levi glances at his watch. "I hate to do this to you, but I've got a woman at home and a daughter who needs tucking into bed." He drops enough cash on the counter for the bartender, to cover our drinks.

Not that I need him picking up my tab. But it's appreciated. I'm not sure I'm capable of counting out a proper tip. Too much booze makes math hard.

Although Julianna would call it *mathing*. The kid likes to turn nouns into verbs.

"See you tomorrow," I mutter as Levi puts on his jacket.

"Let me walk you to the hotel."

"It's just across the street. I can manage myself." I don't need him babysitting me. I'm fine. Well, minus the heart-crushed anger rippling through me. Otherwise, I'm just dandy.

"We're all paid up. I'm walking you home." Levi grabs my coat off the back of the barstool and hands it to me when I stand.

I'm good with my balance, unlike that hot brunette who kept falling all over herself around me. Maybe I'm the reason that she kept tripping, getting all flustered around me.

Although she didn't fall on her face this morning at the interview.

Too bad.

Levi walks me across the street like a child and steps into the foyer with me. "I know you don't want to hear this, but we're friends. Put your differences aside and hire Cali. She's good for the resort."

Why the hell did he have to bring up *her*? Just when my night was finally looking up. "I can take it from here. I don't need a chaperone. Go home to your nanny," I say with a smirk.

"Yes, sir," Levi jokes, and heads back outside.

I glance toward the elevators. I could head upstairs to my room and clean out the mini bar, but what fun would that be? I need a distraction, and another drink is the right answer. Especially after his little speech about that brunette.

I head to the hotel bar and exhale a heavy breath when I see her at the bar counter, sat on a stool. She's nursing a soda, or it could be something like a rum and coke. I don't know what she prefers to drink.

I don't know much about her.

"Is this seat taken?" I grab the stool beside her and sit my ass on it, whether she wants me to or not.

Cali shifts on the stool. An eyebrow raises when she realizes it's me. Maybe she thought it was some other loser going to hit on her.

"I didn't think you'd want to drink with me," Cali says. She gestures the bartender over but frowns.

Does she smell the liquor on my breath? We're rather close, and the bar is mostly empty. I could have chosen anywhere else to sit, but I decided to torture myself by sitting next to her.

Agony.

I should walk away. Leave her alone to suffer without me.

I've punished myself enough as it is, regretting everything about our time together. I want to hate her, but I hate myself even more.

"You're a real witch," I say, gesturing the bartender over. "I'll have a bourbon." My eyes burn, and the room sways slightly, but I'm still on the barstool. I'm not done. Not so long as Cali is sitting beside me at the bar.

"I deserve that," Cali says. She's quiet, soft-spoken. Not like how I remember her. There was a passion in her eyes, a heat in her cheeks, especially when we kissed and I grazed my lips over her body.

The memories with her enslave me.

I gulp the bourbon and gesture for another.

"It's not even the shit you said about me that pisses me off. It's that you involved my kid and her friend," I seethe. "What kind of a monster does that?"

Her gaze moves from me to her drink, studying it like it'll produce the world's answers and solve everything, including world hunger. Well, guess what, Cali, your silence is answer enough.

Acceptance.

Agreement.

She doesn't fight me or argue her side of the story.

"You have nothing to say?" I spit.

"You're drunk, Logan. Now isn't the time to have a deep and meaningful conversation."

"When is the time? Before we fuck?" I ask, growling at her. "Because you assured me that I had nothing to worry about, and then you screwed me over. You tried destroying my company, and worse, my daughter and her friend. Was that fun for you? Mess with a billionaire's family, and let him pick up the pieces by trying to buy away her heartache? Newsflash. That's not how life works."

Cali digs into her purse, puts a twenty on the bar counter and then swings her legs off the barstool. "I'm not doing this with you."

"Not doing what? Being honest?" I retort. "You're good at the lies, Cali. You've made that abundantly clear. How did you get Levi to interview you? What connections do you have? Or were you trying to destroy me from the inside out?"

"You're drunk," Cali says, and grabs her coat. She heads out of the bar, her heels clicking over the wooden floorboards.

I drop cash on the counter for my drink. I should let her go, leave her alone, and sleep off the alcohol.

But I can't stop myself.

My self-control flew out the window hours ago. I'm currently on a train of self-destruction and heading straight for Cali Town.

I hurry out of the bar, my feet slipping on the floor when it changes from wood to marble. But I catch myself before I make a bigger ass out of myself.

The good news is that no one knows who I am around here. I used to live in New York, but I'm not a media highlight. Levi always had more media coverage than I did. I don't envy him for that. It can't be easy.

Cali heads for the elevators, and I follow her, several paces behind. She's already pressed the button to go up, but the elevator car hasn't arrived yet. Three elevators go up twenty to forty flights, but they seem to be slow.

"Please tell me you're going to your room," Cali says.

It's just the two of us. There are plenty of people around, but no one else is waiting by the elevators. I should be grateful that we can have our own brand of privacy, but I'm not happy.

"I'm not done. Why are you here?"

Cali pinches the bridge of her nose. "Not that it's any of your business, but I'm staying at this hotel because I came to New York for a job interview."

I know that. I'm drunk, not an idiot. "Not that," I say, and grimace when I shake my head. "Why Luxenberg Enterprises? What happened in California?" I need to hear it from her lips.

The harder part, however, will be remembering it tomorrow.

TWELVE

Cali

LOGAN NEVER RETURNED MY CALLS. I suspect he blocked my number. I wrote him a letter, which got returned, and he hadn't opened it.

And now he wants an explanation? I've been trying to give him one for the past several weeks, bordering on two months. It's clear he wanted nothing to do with me.

What changed?

I'm frustrated. Tired. And regretting the decision to come to New York. At least I didn't move here. It was just a lousy job interview. I'll return home and keep looking for another job.

"What happened at *Vacationer's Paradise*? Was it not such a paradise?" he retorts.

He's drunk, and I have half a mind not to give in to his questions and ignore him. I'm ready to go up to my room, waiting for the elevator to come, and sleep off the shitty day that I've had. Tomorrow, I'll fly home and never think about Logan Henderson again.

But it's hard not thinking about him.

I screwed him over, and even though it wasn't my fault and Bridget was behind the video and posting the nasty review, I'm weighed down with guilt.

I'm drowning in the bottom of the ocean, refusing to take my last breath. Instead, I let the water and current drag me down to the dark floor of the sea.

"Well?" Logan tilts his head, eyes wide, as he waits for me to respond.

"I got fired," I say, and exhale a breath of relief when the elevator doors open.

I'm not so relieved when he follows right behind me.

I ignore him, push the button for the floor, and hope he'll do the same and we can end this conversation as quickly as it began.

"I'm not surprised," he says, staring at me, straight into my soul. His back is to the elevator doors, and he hasn't pushed any buttons for the floors. But he sure knows how to push my buttons. "After that review you wrote, you should have been fired."

My jaw drops. I shouldn't be surprised he thinks I was behind the appalling review of the resort, but I had nothing to do with it. I was fired before Bridget finalized the video review and posted it.

"First of all, I didn't get fired for that video review. I was fired because I created something nice about your little resort and Bridget got up in arms about me giving another five-star glowing review. Second, Bridget never intended for the resort to get a positive review. She sent me there as punishment because she knows how much I despise the cold. She was hoping that her plan would work, and I'd give you a shitty review."

Logan sways, his hands bunch into fists, and I contemplate putting my arms out to make sure he doesn't fall. But that takes too much energy, and he catches his footing before stumbling.

The elevator dings as we reach my intended destination.

Logan doesn't move. He stands there, staring at me, and I shuffle around him, stepping out of the elevator.

I don't glance back at him to see if he follows.

There's no sound of his shoes clambering or heavy breathing, because it's apparent he's angry with me. I'm surprised he didn't chase me to my room to argue and tell me everything is my fault.

I don't blame him for hating me.

I hate myself for falling into Bridget's trap, believing her to be a good person. That was my mistake, not seeing the signs, the bright neon overhead flashing and warning me to get out while I still had my pride.

And while I still had a chance with Logan.

I shuffle into my hotel room, shut and lock the door, dropping my purse on a nearby end table.

My phone buzzes inside in my purse. It's a text.

I ignore it. More than likely it's junk, something I don't even need to see.

I remove my black heels and unzip my dress, wanting to wear something comfortable after the day I just had.

A second text comes through, or maybe it's the first one reminding me I haven't checked it.

Another buzz.

No, definitely two texts.

Sighing, I grab my phone from my purse and stare back at the text. Apparently, Logan must have unblocked me. At least long enough to send two messages.

I hate you.

Well, I didn't need a text to tell me how he feels.

My stomach lurches when I read the second text.

I can't stop thinking about you. Fuck, I'm falling in love, and you're destroying me.

I grab my pajamas from my luggage and slip on a pair of long flannel bottoms and a long-sleeved shirt.

I shouldn't answer Logan. He's not in his right mind and I'm confident anything I say will only add fuel to an already rampant fire.

But my heart won't stop pounding wildly at his admission that he's falling in love with me. I grimace and grab my phone, texting him back.

You're drunk. Don't say things you're going to regret in the morning. Good night.

I don't expect him to answer, and I certainly don't think we'll see each other tomorrow or ever again. It's more than likely that he'll block me as a contact again, if he hasn't already.

My phone pings once again.

We need to talk. Room number?

He sounds more sober, but that's just the fact there's no tone in a text. That, and he's not rambling and slurring his words.

I take a moment to consider letting him know my room number. I shouldn't indulge this little fantasy of mine. One of us making up, and me bringing him into my bed, moaning his name until the early hours of the morning.

I type my room number and then quickly erase it. *We'll talk when you're sober.* I click send and my fingers tap nervously against the phone screen, waiting for his response.

Bullshit. Room number?

I exhale a heavy breath. That's more like I'd expect. He's angry with me. I deserve his wrath, but I'm not fighting with him.

I ignore his text.

But that doesn't stop him from sending another.

I'll knock on every door on the thirty-third floor. I can wake everyone, or you can let me in so we can talk.

Go to hell.

I shouldn't be so mean. He's hurt. I'm hurt. This is a recipe for disaster.

Down the hall, he's starting with the first door that he reaches when he exits the elevator. I'm only a few rooms down, but he's heading in the wrong direction.

"Cali, we need to talk!" Logan says, pounding on the door.

I can't hear if there's a response, but I imagine someone is telling him either they have the wrong room or they're calling security.

He keeps knocking loudly on doors, refusing to give up. He's going to get his ass thrown out of the hotel. And he'll probably blame me for it.

Reluctantly, I open the room door and poke my head out. "Logan, I'm down here."

He huffs and mutters something to a gentleman who opened the room door for him. Logan stalks down the hall, coming toward my room, and stands outside the door. "Can I come in?"

I'm surprised that he's even asking.

He smells of booze. His eyes are glassy and red, but he's still standing.

I step aside, letting him into the hotel room. I shut the door behind him and fold my arms across my chest. "Now that you've woken the entire hotel, what do you want?" I ask.

"It wasn't the entire hotel," he shoots back. His gaze moves over my body. "You changed."

"I'm not wearing heels and a dress to bed." I plug my phone in, to charge it for the morning, when Logan steps closer, stealing every inch of my personal space, claiming it for his own.

"That's too bad," he growls, and his gaze is filled with hunger, like he hasn't eaten in months.

"What do you want?" I ask, and this time I try to keep my tone calm and civil. There's no point in starting the next world war over Mountain Grump not getting his way.

He expels a heavy breath, his gaze on my lips.

For a moment, I want to will him to say *you*. But that doesn't happen. His eyes tighten and flinch. "I hate you."

My stomach clenches and I tug my bottom lip between my teeth, biting down, trying to keep the tears from surfacing. "I know," I say, like it doesn't hurt, and I don't care. Except that's a lie.

"I hate how you make me feel. Like there's a gaping hole inside of me. A void that you left behind. Your betrayal still rocks me, and I want to move on and forget you ever existed."

"Then why are you here in my room?" I ask.

"Because you're the best candidate for the job."

I take a step back, gliding into the wall.

Trapped.

"What?" I say, unsure I heard him correctly. There's no chance I'm getting hired when he'll end up being my boss. He hates me. I hurt him. Destroyed his company, as he so eloquently put it, and now he wants to hire me. No. He's playing games with me. Trying to get even.

"I hate it, but you're the most qualified and the best vlogger that I've seen. Your content is good. Even when it's shitty, it's good. Fuck," Logan growls.

"I didn't make the negative ad about your resort. You have to believe me."

"I don't believe anything you say." Logan presses one hand against the wall, confining me.

I inhale a sharp breath. My heart slams against my ribcage. The world around me goes fuzzy and blurry, but I focus on the man in front of me with his dark eyes, heated stare, and beard that's close enough to graze my cheek.

"A good working relationship requires trust. Communication." I want him to realize that offering me the job is the worst idea in the world.

No, the worst thing would be taking it.

I can still turn him down. Tell him no thanks and that I don't work for grumpy billionaires who own resorts and live in the mountains.

His gaze flinches. "I won't block your number if that's what you're worried about."

"I'd be reporting to you," I say, staring up at him. How does he not see this as a problem?

"Good. Someone needs to keep your ass in line. And anything you post has to be sent to me first."

That isn't the worst requirement. He's probably hiring me to make sure I don't post anything else negative about the resort, although I never posted the original video, either. I run a hand through my hair and he grabs my arm, pinning it to the wall.

"Don't be nervous. Unless you have something to hide, *Sunshine*."

I inhale a sharp breath. He hasn't called me that in quite some time. It doesn't feel quite so fitting, with anger bubbling at the surface. It's like a game of cat and mouse. And he's ready to pounce.

I'm just not sure if I'll be eaten or ravished.

"Like I told you, that video, the one on the vlog, isn't mine."

"Good. And you should know, if you work for me, and you will," he says with confidence like he's already drafted the papers and waiting for me to sign on the dotted line, "everything you film becomes property of Luxenberg Enterprises. All of it is accessible to me and you will only be allowed to film using a company phone."

That doesn't sound horribly unreasonable. "Everything I film will be with the company phone," I say.

"Everything you film, period. If you take a shot of my tattoos, my face, a clip of me getting coffee, it belongs to me. I decide what gets released and what gets destroyed."

I exhale a shaky breath.

Is he being unreasonable?

"I never said I accepted the position."

"But you will," Logan says with self-assurance that leaves me weak at the knees. His gaze is latched on mine. The man is smug. "One other thing," he says, and drops his hold on my arm, letting me free but not giving me space to move without pushing physically past him.

The wall seems to be the only thing holding me up at the moment.

"The contract will stipulate that you are to live on the property, but you aren't to bring anyone home with you."

"Excuse me?"

"You will be focused on your work, Ms. Sinclair. I don't need you chasing after the next hot young ass that interests you. That's not what I'm paying you for."

He's not technically paying me anything, yet.

"Is that a problem?" He stares at me, and the air leaves my lungs before I can answer.

Wordlessly, I shake my head.

"I need verbal confirmation, Ms. Sinclair."

"It's not a problem," I say. My voice is shaky and unreliable. Damn him for having the power to make my knees like jelly and my insides toasty.

I clear my throat, trying to gain some semblance of control.

"But I haven't accepted the position yet, Mr. Henderson," I say, using the same formality he's using. However, nothing we're doing is quite formal. I'm in my pajamas, and he has me trapped against the wall, his breath caressing my skin.

"You wouldn't have come all the way to New York unless you were desperate."

I refuse to acknowledge his accusation. "You can have your office send me over a formal offer, and I will decide what is in my best interest."

His top lip twitches before he snarls and leans in. I swear he's going to kiss me. I hold my breath, and my eyes fall to his lips. The moment drags on and my body tingles with anticipation. The heat of his mouth hovers, teasing, making me lean in before he pulls away and turns for the door.

Not another word is spoken.

He heads out of the hotel room, leaving me gasping for breath with my heart racing and my body trembling.

————

It all happens so fast, the offer letter, the acceptance, and packing a bag for my trip back to Breckenridge.

I shouldn't have accepted the offer, but the pay is exceptional, and the cost of living is drastically less. Especially when I factor in that I'm staying at the resort.

Although I don't think it's a permanent requirement, they're providing me a room free of charge.

Logan and Levi insist that I begin first thing Monday morning. I have enough time to pack for a few weeks and the rest of my apartment is getting boxed up and packed by professional movers, at the expense of Luxenberg Enterprises.

While I don't technically work for Logan and he's not the one signing my checks, he is the one who handles every operation of the work I do. It's complicated. Frustrating. And sleeping with him again is out of the question.

He hates me.

Hell, some days I hate myself.

I've yet to see Julianna. She's in school during the day, and I'm not sure if she's avoiding me in the evenings or just isn't around the resort.

I owe her an apology, although if she's anything like her father, she'll ignore me and continue to hate my guts.

The tension is thick, and I spend what time I can away from Logan. He has his own office and mine is down the hall. It's not particularly far from him, but I spend quite a bit of my time taking photos, video, and creating different types of content to spruce up the resort.

I want to discuss with Logan about updating the website, not just the social media profiles, but I'm not sure he'll be receptive to my ideas.

I knock on his open door, and he doesn't so much as glance up at me. "Yes?"

"I have some footage to show you," I say.

He finally glances up and gestures for me to sit across from him. There's no smile on his face. His eyes are dark, weary. The man looks like he hasn't slept since that night in New York. Possibly longer.

I walk him through accessing the videos saved to the cloud where he can view the creative content in addition to all original files. Anything that is saved to the phone automatically gets copied to the cloud.

His face is stoic. And I'm not sure whether he hates it or just hates me. If he liked it, he'd tell me and smile. His features might even soften.

"Is this all you've done?" Logan asks.

My eyes widen, and I straighten my back. "No, Mr. Henderson. I've also taken photographs and created a mock version of a new website that I think might be beneficial. We can collect email addresses and offer a coupon for guests' first night if they stay longer than three nights."

Slowly, he nods, like he might actually not hate the idea.

"What else?"

I suck in a nervous breath. "While I haven't posted anything to our social media accounts without your approval, I made sure they are updated with the relevant contact information."

"And that wasn't the case?"

"Someone had put the wrong phone number and address on all the sites," I say.

Logan frowns and pulls up the Twitter account first, verifying that I didn't mess everything up.

Why can't he believe me?

When he's satisfied the information is accurate, he checks every individual account where Blue Sky Resort has a social media presence.

"Wonderful," he mutters, but he doesn't sound the least bit happy. "What else?"

"I have several mockup videos that I've made and are ready to be posted, along with a few games and giveaways to get our account growing." I walk him through where the information is located, and he peruses it before glancing back at me. "Is there anything else you'd like?" I ask.

"Other than to get Bridget to remove the scathing vlog post on *Vacationer's Paradise*?"

It seems he plans to hold that against me for all of eternity. Although I haven't been working here that long, there's still time to prove myself an asset.

"I can give her a call and talk with her?" I offer, not that I think she'll want to talk to me. She fired me.

"Don't, my lawyers are all over it," Logan says. He finally meets my stare. "You've done a lot, but we haven't seen an increase in reservations or bookings."

"It takes time for our marketing efforts to work, Mr. Henderson," I say, trying to keep things as professional as possible. "And I need your approval to start posting content, which I hope will result in the increase that you're hoping to see. I might also suggest that we run campaign ads."

"Campaign ads?"

"Cost per click campaigns with sites like Google and Facebook. We might even try running a video ad on one of the streaming apps."

His gaze tightens. "You have all sorts of ways to spend my money, Ms. Sinclair. How about let's come up with ways to generate income from new revenue streams that won't cost me an arm and a leg?"

That's what I've done. Not that he sees it. "Of course, I will do some research and get back with you," I say, trying to get out before he loses his temper. It's coming, I can feel the rage and hatred ready to spew.

I'm relieved when he dismisses me from his office, and I can scurry back to my desk and avoid his heated wrath.

What I don't expect is to see Wyatt in my office, seated at my desk.

"Can I help you?" I ask, glancing him over.

He's stretched out, feet on my desk, arms behind his head. "Just hiding from the boss," Wyatt quips.

"Can you do that someplace else?"

Wyatt moves out of my chair from behind the desk but doesn't leave my office. "This is the only sanctuary from Logan."

What is he talking about? I frown, shaking my head, waiting for him to elaborate.

"Logan can't stand being around you. He's not going to willy nilly show up in your office. Which means I can chill for two minutes without him jumping down my throat."

"Is that what you're doing? Chilling?" I ask. I step around to the chair that he had recently occupied and take my seat behind the desk. Unlike Wyatt, my feet aren't up on the desk and I'm not lounging around taking a cat nap or whatever the hell he intended to do before I caught him.

"Avoiding work. Chilling. Same difference," Wyatt says. He's quiet, staring at me as he plops down on the nearby sofa against the wall. "How'd Logan convince you to come back and work for him?"

"He didn't tell you?" I ask, my fingers poised over the keys on the keyboard.

"That man has been a grump since the moment you left. He barely talks to anyone about anything. Unless he's throwing out orders and commands like he's back in the service."

"I didn't realize he was in the military."

"He doesn't talk about it much," Wyatt says.

"For what it's worth, I'm glad you're back. Even if you are the queen of betrayal."

I grimace. "Is that what Logan said?" I ask. Did I inherit that nickname when I left the first time?

"It's kind of obvious. I'm not sure why you'd be crazy enough to come back here when you think this place is run like a shit show and not worth a night's stay."

"I didn't write those terrible things in the video," I say.

Wyatt's gaze tightens. "Who did?"

"Bridget Lancaster, my former boss."

He strokes his jaw and nods slowly. "Let me guess, you quit after she changed your video and posted it on their social media feed?"

"I was fired when she saw that I gave the resort five stars."

His brow tightens. "I don't get it."

"Yeah, me either. Apparently, Bridget sent me to the mountains as punishment and expected a scathing review. When I didn't deliver, she axed me and finished the job herself."

Wyatt presses his lips together, grabs his phone from his pocket and opens TikTok, searching for *Vacationer's Paradise*. He exhales a whistle when he sees video after video of negative reviews on a multitude of locations.

"We should take this bitch down," Wyatt says.

"I'm pretty sure your brother has his attorney already on the situation."

"No, like Bridget needs to be taken down," Wyatt repeats. "You don't understand; this woman has been a menace from the beginning. She's best friends with his ex-wife. There's a lot of history between them."

"Ancient history," Logan says when he walks by and overhears part of the conversation. "Why are we discussing Bridget?"

"Have you seen the shit she's done to other resorts?" Wyatt leaps up from the sofa and shoves his phone in Logan's face. "The woman is a menace. We might be able to push a class action suit—"

"Shut it!" Logan growls at his brother. "We're not pushing anything. It's better if Bridget buries herself in stupid videos that no one watches. Leave it alone."

"We can't," Wyatt says, unable to stop himself from letting it go. "Have you seen how many views her account has? Apparently, being mean makes you viral."

"I don't care. Not another word about *her*," Logan seethes. At least his anger is no longer directed at me and is instead at the woman I used to work for. A woman from his past.

———

I swear Logan avoids me the rest of the week, except when we're discussing business matters like content to post. He gives me his approval without a smile or a hint of pleasure in what he does.

He's the master of all that is grumpy. And I'm constantly tiptoeing around the man, which is annoying as hell.

Why did I do this to myself? Agree to work under the man who hates me?

There were other ways to punish myself that didn't involve Mountain Grump. I can't get his heated stare out of my head from when he was in the hotel room with me.

I should have kissed him. Our lips were close enough that I could practically feel his touch.

Maybe then I could have warmed his heart of ice.

I'm off the clock at five, and I leave the resort and take a local shuttle bus that takes guests from the resort to the shopping district and back.

My head swims, and my stomach has been bloated like I'm about to burst. I head for the nearest drug store, because when I do the math, I should have had my period four weeks ago and I'm way beyond late.

I'm fucked.

I cannot be pregnant.

There were pregnancy tests at the resort in the gift shop, but I'm not taking a chance that anyone I work with will see me buy the test.

And if I'm pregnant, what then?

There's only one man I've slept with in the past two months: Logan Henderson. If I'm pregnant, undoubtedly, it's his child.

I can't let my mind wander beyond that scenario itself. It's terrifying. Nauseating. I want to throw myself off the moving bus and would sooner get hit by traffic than face the fact that the man who is now my boss might also be the father of my unborn child.

Well, he doesn't write my paychecks, but I do report to him.

Talk about confusing.

After twenty minutes of driving out of town away from the lodge, we pull up to the shopping district. There are a bunch of small retail shops, a drug store, and a grocery store.

I head to the drug store and stalk inside, grabbing the first one on the shelf that promises to be the most accurate, and take it up to the cashier.

As she's ringing up my order, Julianna and her friend step up in line behind me with a handful of sugary sweets, chocolate, and glass bottles of flavored soda.

"Hi, Jules," I say, hoping the cashier can shove the pregnancy test into the bag before the teen notices what I'm buying. "I'm sorry about—"

She cuts me off before I can continue.

"Don't worry about it," she says casually. Her eyes land on the counter, and she raises a curious eye. "You've been busy."

I open my mouth to snap at her not to judge me and that this could very well be her half-sibling when the clerk tells me the total and asks how I'll be paying for it today.

I grab my credit card from my purse and tap the card reader, wanting the nightmare to be over.

Except this is only the beginning.

And while I haven't taken the test yet, I'm never late. I'm always on time and the fluttery feeling in my stomach and the nausea that's been hitting me every morning isn't only because I have to face Logan every day.

I already know the results and I haven't even peed on the stick yet.

THIRTEEN

Logan

JULIANNA COMES RUNNING into my office with Izzie on her heels. They shut the door, indicating that they want privacy with me. "Is everything okay?" I ask.

Izzie stares at Julianna, waiting for her to speak.

My daughter has a reusable shopping bag slung over her shoulder.

"Did something happen at the store?" I ask. I can't help but worry, and my hands tighten into fists as I stand.

"Yes, but Izzie and I are fine," Julianna quickly says, dismissing my concern. "It's Cali."

"What about Cali?" I'm not sure I want to know, but if something happened to her, she's my best talent around here. Not that I'm willing to admit that aloud.

"We caught her buying a pregnancy test at the drug store," Julianna says.

"You did?" I shouldn't care. It doesn't matter. Cali and I haven't been together since before Christmas. My eyes widen and I exhale a heavy breath. "Did she say anything?" I ask.

Who the hell is she dating?

Or is it some random guy she slept with?

I wince. Is that what I am to her? Just another random guy in her long string of men whom she likes to toy with and use?

"Not a word. It was pretty obvious she was embarrassed, though. And I mean, Dad, you totally sell those tests in the gift store behind the clerk. She didn't have to go all the way into town."

Unless she didn't want anyone she works with to know she's pregnant.

"Listen, whatever is going on with Cali, that's her business. We don't discuss it. Okay?"

"You mean we don't discuss it in front of her," Julianna says. "Right?"

"No, we don't discuss it at all," I clarify. Why does my daughter think it's okay to be talking about Cali and whether or not she's pregnant? "She's my employee. Any further conversation would be highly inappropriate."

"Right. So, I can't ask her if the results are positive?"

She isn't serious. "You're kidding, right?" I can't take my daughter's sense of humor right now. The thought that another man touched Cali, fucked her, makes my stomach churn. No man should be anywhere near her.

"Got it. That topic is off-limits. By the way, I'm glad Cali is back, even if you're still an old grump!" She grabs Izzie's arm and drags her friend out of my office. I'm relieved when I'm alone and don't have to deal with the two teens. Although I do take Julianna's earlier suggestion seriously.

While she wants an arcade, I'm not interested in policing dozens of teens. I am, however, willing to splurge and create a private game room for Julianna and her friends. But I don't intend on telling her until the place is ready, and I can surprise her with it.

I finish up for the night, close up my office and head to the lodge to check on staff and our guests. I could go upstairs and relax in front of the television, but I can't sit still.

Not with the news that Cali might be pregnant.

I haven't exactly been easy on her since she moved here, but she hasn't been back in Breckenridge long enough to get knocked up and pregnant. At least not to the point that the pregnancy would give a positive result.

What does that mean for me?

If she's pregnant, then it has to be with someone in Los Angeles. Will she plan on leaving the first opportunity she gets?

I grab my phone and dial Levi. This isn't something I can talk to Wyatt about. He'd be over the moon, probably tell me that I should step up and help her out. No thanks. The two of us can barely be in the same room together.

"This better be good," Levi answers.

"Julianna caught Cali buying a pregnancy test." Is that good enough for him to pull him away from his perfect life for five minutes?

"Aww shit. Hold on a sec." He covers the phone, probably tells Clare that he has to take this call. There's rustling and movement and then silence on the other end. "I'm back. Are you sure the test is for herself?"

"Cali doesn't exactly have many friends in Breckenridge," I say. She hasn't been here long enough to make friends, at least, as far as I've noticed.

"So, it's some guy from back home."

"Probably," I mutter, and slink into a comfy chair in the lodge. The place is pretty sparse, and while there are a few guests at a table, I'm far enough away that no one hears my conversation.

I should retreat to my office, but I don't want to feel so confined right now. That room is suffocating after the kind of bombshell my daughter dropped. But thankfully, it's not Julianna who's pregnant. I couldn't handle that kind of news.

This doesn't affect me. Other than I might lose a decent employee. Not that I've been particularly nice or easy on her. She has no reason to stay in town, and while the job pays well, I'm sure whoever the father is will step up and take care of her and the child.

She'll probably never have to work another day in her life.

"Didn't you sleep with her?" Levi asks.

"That was ages ago," I say.

"Right." Levi doesn't push the suggestion, and I'm glad, because there's no way it's my kid. I used a condom, and it was weeks ago. Like long enough that she should have noticed already. I run a hand through my hair, those thoughts making me uncomfortable.

"What's the problem?" Levi asks. "Are you worried she's going to bail on the new gig? We can find someone else. I know you liked her work, but there are other talented creators out there."

"I can't believe she slept with someone else," I growl. My fingers dig into the armrest, scratching the leather.

"You two seemed pretty broken up to me, when I met her."

"Not helping," I grumble at him.

"Didn't you tell me that you blocked her number, and the letter she sent, you had returned without opening the envelope?"

Why does he have to remember every little detail? "That's beside the point."

"Is it?" Levi asks. "Because what were you expecting from her? If she was going to apologize, she'd have called you, texted, or sent you a letter via post. All of which you declined."

"She could have flown here to see me and explain things." I exhale a heavy breath and lean forward. I need to keep my shit together, or people are going to start looking at me and wondering what the hell is wrong.

"Is that what you wanted? Would you have even spoken with her?" Levi asks.

He's right. I'd have probably sent her away, but she didn't even try to come and visit me. "I might have," I say.

"Bullshit. You would have sent her home, and I know girls like Cali. They can't afford to fly last minute, especially when they were just fired from their previous place of employment."

"Fuck," I growl, hating that Levi is right.

"You have two options. Treat her like a professional and let her live her life the way she wants or step up your game and offer to be there for her, no strings attached. She may surprise you."

That's the problem. Cali always has a way of surprising me, and it usually leaves me feeling breathless and ill at ease. "You're suggesting I be a daddy to her kid?" I can't believe Levi. He's suddenly fallen into the role of being a father and taking it quite seriously.

"No, just be supportive. If the father doesn't step up and come into the picture, she's going to need help. Especially if she stays in Breckenridge. She doesn't know anyone, right?"

I groan under my breath. "I'm forty-three, Levi. I'm done with diapers and sleepless nights from newborns. I went through all that already when I had Julianna."

"No one is saying that you have to play daddy to the kid. But Cali might need a friend, and I know you still have feelings for her."

Why does he think that he knows me so well? "I don't." It's a lie. I don't want to have feelings for Cali, but they don't seem to just disappear because I want them to go away.

Why is that?

Why has she managed to irritate me to no end and make me crave her body like it belongs to me? I've never felt that way about anyone before, not even my ex-wife, Jess.

"Keep telling yourself that," Levi says. "Clare and I didn't always have a perfect relationship. We had our own issues to overcome. Just think of this as a test. If you both survive and don't kill each other, maybe you'll grow stronger together."

I grumble under my breath. "I didn't call looking for love advice. And I'm sure that we'll murder each other long before we can ever fall in love."

"That sounds like one hell of a tragedy," Levi says. "You really should get out more. Get laid. If Cali isn't the girl, find someone who is and just keep things professional with her. Listen, I have to go. Amelia found me and is climbing me like a jungle gym and Clare seems to have disappeared."

"Sounds about right."

"Keep me updated," Levi says.

I hang up the call and glance back at the happy table of customers in the lounge. What started out as chit chat has turned to a friendly game of cards.

I walk past the older gentleman, probably in his mid-sixties, who gestures toward me. "Do you want to join us?" he offers.

"No, but thank you." I contemplate sitting down with the table, asking them what they like and don't like with the resort for some honest and genuine feedback. But I don't think I could stomach any more bad news.

Cali being pregnant is enough to make me want to slam my head into a wall. I head up a flight of stairs for the fitness room.

I need to let off steam and a run a few miles on the treadmill. It's a better option than jogging outside where it's freezing, and the forecast is calling for snow overnight.

But the entire time I'm running, all I can think about is Cali. Her smile. Her laugh. That nose twitch when she gets upset with me before lashing out.

I run faster and harder, but she's still in my head, and when I'm done working out, I head upstairs for a cold shower. The icy cold water is cruel and only makes my body ache further. I turn the water hot, imagining Cali's mouth kissing a path down to my cock.

I don't want to fantasize about her, but I can't stop myself from thinking about what it would be like to plow into her sassy little mouth. I stroke my shaft, wishing it was her lips and tongue on me, taking every inch as I silence her and make her obey.

The longer I last, the more I wish I had her here in the shower, pinned between me and the wall. After she takes me in her mouth, I'd take her in the shower, pressed against the cold tile, and watch her nipples harden. I'd suck each mound while fucking her until she screams my name. And only then, would I let her come.

But that's all I get from Cali, a fantasy that I dream up.

I finish off in the shower, dry off, and change into a pair of cargos and a T-shirt. I can't be wandering around the lodge in my boxers, and I'm too tired to bother with putting on anything more professional. Besides, this is a ski lodge. We're not a palace.

Stepping out of the bedroom, I see Cali is on my sofa, her feet tucked up beneath her. "How'd you get in?" I ask, surprised to see her.

"Jules let me inside. I told her I needed to talk with you. I was kind of surprised that she didn't tell me to go to hell."

Me too. I glance her over. I can't visibly see that she's pregnant, but I can't imagine why else she'd be up here tonight. "This is about work?" I guess. She'll probably need more time off and, of course, maternity leave.

"Umm, not really," Cali says. She emits a heavy sigh and gently pats the sofa beside her. She wants me to come and sit.

"I already know you're pregnant," I say. "How long did you wait before sleeping with someone else after me? Was I just an empty fuck? A placeholder until you met the next guy who you wanted to screw over?" I shouldn't be so callous, but the words spill out faster than I intend.

Her brow pinches, and her lips part. Those perfect ruby lips, that I envisioned sucking my cock, will never come anywhere near it if it were up to her. I've destroyed any chance at the two of us being anything beyond friends.

It wasn't as though I intended to hurt her, but with the bickering we've been doing, and the pain that I can't seem to erase, this is what we've become.

Cali emits a heavy sigh. "Julianna told you she saw me at the store today."

"Yes." There's no sense in lying to her. "I take it the test came back positive."

She laughs darkly under her breath. "Oh, I'm pregnant, and in case you haven't figured it out yet, the kid is yours." She pins me with her stare.

I swear the air is sucked right out of my lungs. I shake my head, denial the only feeling that seems to be real. The room spins, and I sink into the sofa, leaving an extra couch cushion between us.

"Mine?" My voice squeaks, and I grimace at the sound of my uncertainty. "Are you sure?"

"One hundred percent. But when I make a doctor's appointment to verify the pregnancy, we can discuss verifying the paternity as well if you don't believe me."

I'm not sure what to believe. The room is spinning, and I take several long and deep breaths to focus.

"I'm the father?" It's the only thought I can make sense of in the chaos she's thrown at me. "Are you sure there's no one else? We slept together months ago."

"Two months," Cali says. "And between the stress of getting fired and moving, I didn't even think about the fact that I missed my period until earlier today. And no, for the record, unless my vibrator can suddenly get a girl pregnant. You're the only guy I've been with in quite a while."

"You didn't sleep with Wyatt?" Not that I really thought she fucked my brother, but that night at the bar, when she was having drinks with him, I still feel the burn of jealousy.

"I don't screw every man who buys me a drink. Give me some credit."

I should apologize, but I don't. We're too far past that point to fix things between us.

"What do you plan on doing?" I ask.

"Am I going to keep it?" Cali stares at me, her fingers graze over the fabric of her pants. She's nervous and for good reason. This isn't easy on either of us. "Yes, and I'd like to stay in Breckenridge, assuming I still have a job."

Her remark cuts me deep. "Do you think I'd fire you after knocking you up?"

"Well, when you put it like that," Cali says, and brings her knees to her chest, wrapping her arms around them. She rests her chin on her legs. "I honestly had no idea how you'd react."

She looks so young, vulnerable, and conflicted.

And I'm the one to blame. No one else hurt her. I did that, all on my own. Not that she's innocent, but if what she's been spieling is the truth, maybe I've been a bit more of an ass toward her than I need to be.

"Your job isn't going anywhere. When you have to take maternity leave, we'll deal with it. We have a while until that happens," I say, assuring her that her job isn't a problem.

"Good," she says, and her shoulders slouch. She looks so small and fragile.

I pull her into my lap, and she inhales sharply, her body frozen and rigid.

"Relax," I growl into her ear. "I'm not going to bite."

After a few seconds, she seems to relax, at least a little.

"We need to get you set up with an OBGYN. I'm guessing that you don't have a doctor already in town."

Cali quietly shakes her head.

"We'll find you one of the best physicians. I'm sure they'll verify the pregnancy as well," I say.

What are the chances it's a false positive?

Will I be disappointed if I found she isn't pregnant and this is all a mistake?

My hands roam up and down her arms, trying to coax her. She's trembling, and I can't tell if it's my doing or the adrenaline from telling me the news.

"Talk to me," I say. "Tell me what you're feeling."

"Nervous. Scared. Terrified." Her gaze isn't on me, and I reach for her chin, tilting her head and forcing her to meet my stare. Her blue eyes are brighter, clearer, but filled with doubt.

I don't ever want her to feel that kind of doubt about us or with me. "I'm sorry," I say. "I realize I've been a hard ass on you." I pull her tighter and rest my forehead against hers.

"It's not your fault."

I laugh softly. "I appreciate that, but I haven't made things any easier on you or on us."

She doesn't argue with me. There's no reason for her to, because she must know I'm right. Cali shifts slightly, resting her head against my chest. I wrap my arms around her, cocooning her in my embrace.

"You're my boss," she whispers against my chest. "This seems like a problem." Cali gestures at her stomach.

"Only if we make it a problem." I rest my chin on the top of her head. "You're having my child." I exhale, trying to let the words sink in. It feels surreal. "Anyways, you work for Levi. I'm just the guy you report to."

She chuckles and rubs at her eyes.

Is she crying?

My thumb swipes across her cheek, wiping the remnants of tears away. "I promise, I won't make your life hell."

"You've already been doing that," Cali mutters. She rubs her face into my chest. "Do you remember that night in New York?"

I stiffen at her recollection of the interview and me being drunk much later that evening. "What about it?"

Apparently, I hadn't consumed enough to make me completely forget what happened, including telling her that I was falling in love with her.

"I really thought you were going to kiss me in my hotel room."

Her words make me relax. I thought she was going to bring up the other thing I had said. "I should have kissed you, but I was drunk and that would have been wrong."

"You're not drunk now, are you?" Cali asks, lifting her gaze back to mine.

"I'm not," I say, and stare at her perfect ruby lips. They're begging me to ravish them. But my daughter is in the next room over with her friend. "But we can't be making out like teenagers on the couch. Julianna is home."

"I know; she let me inside," Cali reminds me.

"What do you suggest we do?" I want to take this little private party to the bedroom, but I don't want to push Cali. It's been quite the day, discovering that she's pregnant and me learning I'm going to be a father again.

I lean my forehead against hers, breathing her scent in. She smells like lavender and vanilla. It takes all my willpower not to run my tongue down her neck and listen to her moan as I excite her.

Cali reaches for my hair, trailing her fingers through my scalp. Her touch is sensual and calming, luring me to kiss her.

There's only so long I can keep up this charade, pretending I don't want to devour every inch of her. And I'm losing fast.

My breath catches when she shifts slightly and leans closer, her breasts grazing my chest. I growl and press my lips hard against hers. I need her like I need air to breathe.

Her lips part, allowing me entrance, and I willfully take what's granted.

She's mine.

The kiss deepens and my fingers tangle in her hair, pulling her harder, closer, tighter. As much as I want to undress her on the couch, there are two teenagers just a room away.

I pull back and Cali whimpers in protest. I don't want her thinking that the kiss is done and that I regret any of it. In a matter of seconds, I lift her into my arms, carrying her to my bedroom.

"I can walk," she says, and squeals, smacking my arm playfully.

"You mean you haven't tripped over your feet this week?"

She sticks out her tongue at me, and I lean in, trying to capture it. Our tongues duel and as I place her on the bed, I climb atop her, straddling her hips.

Cali moans, grinding her hips into mine.

"Slow down, *Sweetheart*," I say. "We've got all night."

My fingers graze the hem of her shirt, and I pull it up and over, helping her undress. As soon as it's discarded, I pounce on her, my mouth trailing a path of warm kisses down her chest as I guide my hands behind her back, unclasping her bra.

She emits a soft sigh when the material slides away and my lips devour her breast. With one nipple in my mouth, sucking and kissing her flesh, my other hand caresses her velvety skin.

Her fingers tug my shirt up and over my head, and it gets momentarily tangled before I release my lips from her breast, lifting off her long enough to discard my shirt and then my pants with it.

My boxers and her panties are the only article of clothing we both wear. And I fully intend on ridding her of her undergarment. My lips move back over her stomach and her fingers tangle in my hair as I whisper my soft apologies.

"I'm so sorry that I blamed you for what happened." I don't want to fight with her ever again.

"Me too," she whispers, reaching down and pulling me back to her face. "I wanted to apologize. I tried, but I should have kept trying."

"I was stubborn. I don't think anything you said would have gotten through this thick skull." I point at my head.

"You're not wrong." Cali leans forward, biting on my bottom lip, tugging it between her teeth with a wicked grin.

I growl at her as she releases her grip on my lip. "Damn, girl, did you just bite me?"

She raises an eyebrow. "You did block my number, *Mountain Grump*." The smirk on her face tugs at my heart. I want to be the one who makes her happy, every day, for the rest of my life. Will she give me that pleasure and let me be there for her and our child?

"And I've learned from my mistakes. I apologize," I say.

"Good. I would hope so." There's a sassiness to her. The same snarkiness that revealed itself when we first met downstairs in the gift shop.

My lips fall back down her body, kissing a wayward trail down south, and I pause over her navel, realizing with an enormity what is growing inside of her.

Our child.

"No matter what, Cali, I'll be there for you and for our baby." I need her to know I'm not abandoning her or letting our differences get in the way of what's happening.

"And if I'm not pregnant and the test is wrong?" Her bright-blue eyes stare up at me. "What happens then?"

"I'll never stop caring about you," I say. I'm not ready to confess my feelings are deeper than just caring about her. The L word feels too heavy right now, and I hope she's not expecting it.

And though it feels like we have a mountain to climb, we'll do it together. We don't have to race, there's no finish line.

EPILOGUE

CALI

40 Weeks Pregnant

I swear I'm going to kill Logan for making me the size of a balloon, and not the type with helium that you see at birthday parties. No, I'm the size of a hot-air balloon about ready to pop at any moment.

That moment is now.

My water broke, and Logan is ushering me to the helicopter pad, because the nearest hospital is two hours away.

And he insists on us having our child at the hospital, not at home with a midwife. He doesn't want to take any chances or risk the life of the child or mother.

I don't argue, but the contractions are hell.

Will I make it to the hospital, or am I about to give birth in his luxury private helicopter? That's not a story I want to tell when our child gets older.

He buckles me into the helicopter seat. Logan is the pilot and while I want to squeeze his hand and feel him there for support, he needs to focus on getting us to the hospital alive.

The flight isn't as awful as I imagined it would be, and before long, I'm being wheeled into the hospital to deliver a baby boy.

"I hate you," I grind between clenched teeth at Logan. The contractions are seconds apart, not minutes. The pain radiates through every inch of me, and I want this baby out.

He takes my hand in the most gentle and soothing manner, and I squeeze the crap out of it as another contraction rips through me.

"I can't believe you talked me into this!" I growl at him.

Logan knows when to keep his mouth shut, and right now, he's trying to contain himself. Whether he's annoyed with me or just biting his lip to keep from making some snide comment, he's wise to remain quiet.

The doctor instructs me to push, and if I thought the pain couldn't get any worse, I was wrong.

I'm exhausted, and our baby hasn't even made it into the world yet. How am I going to handle being a mother?

Worry plagues my mind, and Logan latches onto my palm with both hands, his grip strong. "You've got this, *Sunshine*. You're tough. You can do it. Just breathe through the contractions like we practiced."

"Like I practiced," I snap at him. I can't help the anger that jolts through me. It's worse than our first fight. Except this time, I don't mean it. And the tears fall because I don't want him to hate me.

When did I become such a wreck?

Oh, right, pregnancy.

Hormones and growing a child inside of you will do it.

I'm flooded with relief when the baby is finally born, seven pounds, four ounces. He has Logan's dark hair and my bright-blue eyes. He's healthy and perfect.

We both decide to name him Miles, because Logan swears to me that he'd travel every mile across the world if I ever left his ass again. I vow in return that nothing would ever come between us or stand in our way.

We're not wed, not yet. Some things take more time than others. Our primary focus has been strengthening our relationship and ensuring that Julianna is settling in with a new sibling.

I moved into the penthouse suite a few months after our pregnancy announcement. Having a room at the resort to myself seemed absurd, and Logan wanted to witness every moment of the pregnancy together.

I wanted that, too, with him.

I still work for Luxenberg Enterprises and report up through Logan, which seems crazy, but Levi doesn't have a problem with it as long as we are both productive and the resort is doing well. Plus, I suppose Levi and Logan being business partners makes the issues non-existent. Logan doesn't technically work for Levi.

And Jules finally gets to intern for me when she's out of school this summer. I think Levi might even pay her a few dollars for the gig, but she's more excited to learn everything I do and help run our social media accounts.

Blue Sky Resort has been doing fantastic. We are constantly booked out during the winter months. Logan keeps talking about adding on to the resort and expanding.

I half-expect Logan to buy a car for Julianna's sixteenth birthday. Instead, he set up a game room in one of the empty suites downstairs that requires a private keycard for entry. Whenever Julianna wants to invite her friends over and is looking for something to do, especially in the summer, the game room gets a lot of use.

There are old-school video games like Pac-Man, an array of arcade racing games, and even a claw machine that Logan filled with stuffed animals.

It is quite literally Jules' arcade. The girl doesn't know how lucky she has it with Logan as her father. And I'm sure Miles will be spoiled just as much when he gets older.

Logan brings Miles and me home. He's thought of everything, turning the spare bedroom into a nursery. Although we also have a bassinet set up in the master suite.

I'm stretched out on the sofa, nursing Miles, when Logan grabs a seat beside me. He lifts my legs, sitting under them before putting my feet back on his lap. His fingers instantly move to massage my calves and feet.

The man is a dream come true. I don't know how I got so lucky.

"He looks just like you," Logan says, admiring his son.

"I don't know. I think he looks a lot like you," I whisper with a wayward smile. I don't want to chance waking Miles, since he just fell asleep.

I burp him, and Logan offers to take him and put him down in his bassinet. I hand the sleeping infant over and lean back, letting my eyes drift closed. I'm exhausted, and it's only the first week. At least at the hospital, the nurses were helpful, but now the baby depends on me for survival.

That thought alone scares me.

"He's asleep," Logan says, and climbs right back on the sofa, resuming his earlier position a few minutes prior.

"Oh, good." I can't help but yawn. I can't seem to catch up on sleep, and with a new baby, I wonder when the next time I'll be able to sleep through the night will be. Weeks? Months? It feels daunting.

"Are you okay?" Logan's touch is gentle and soothing as he caresses my legs.

I nod and let my eyes drift closed. "I feel like I could sleep for a week."

I imagine Logan smiling, but I'm too tired to open my eyes.

"Me too," he says with a soft laugh. "But no comparison, you win."

I nudge him with my toes. "It's not a competition," I say. "And thank you for not getting mad at me at the hospital. I'm sorry for all the terrible things I said while in labor. That was awful."

"The things that you said, or the pain?"

I open my eyes, and he's grinning.

"Both," I say. "I love you." I'd felt it for months, but it wasn't something I'd said. I need him to know that nothing will ever come between us.

"I love you too," he whispers, and reaches for the blanket on the sofa. "You should get some rest while Miles is asleep." He pulls the blanket over me, helping me get comfortable.

"You're on diaper duty when he wakes up," I mumble between a yawn.

"It would be my pleasure."

"Liar." He may offer to change Miles' diaper, but I know he doesn't want to. No one wants to change a stinky baby's diaper.

Logan climbs off the sofa and leans down, pressing his lips to my forehead. "For you, Cali, I'd do anything."

And I believe he would, just as I'd do anything for him.

––––––––

Thank you for reading Mountain Grump. I hope you enjoyed Logan and Cali's story. Continue the adventure with Bachelor Grump.

We've all had that nightmare date, the one that makes you want to throw yourself off the platform in front of an oncoming train.

Mine is my hot next-door neighbor who just moved into the building.

He's a bachelor. And while he's gorgeous and easy on the eyes, his mouth needs to be zipped shut.

It's my fault. He asked me out, and I said yes, not knowing that he was an arrogant jerk.

I'd love to say that I'd never see him again, but it gets worse...

He's also my new boss, and I'm his assistant. He overhears me mocking his "junk" to my colleague, and I swear I didn't intend to show my face at the office ever again.

Because Mr. Grump is the ultimate bosshole.

Arrogant.

Demanding.

Manipulative.

I swear he planned it, showing up at the bar, knocking me off my game. And then the bet... there's no going back.

Imagine my surprise when I find out he has a son.

Mr. Grump is a single father. Boy, do I feel bad for the kid.

This steamy romantic comedy is an enemies-to-lovers romance. It is a standalone, with no cheating, no cliffhanger, and a happily ever after ending.

One-click Bachelor Grump now!

———

Sign up for Willow Fox's newsletter

And I'm thrilled to offer a sneak peek of Bachelor Grump featuring Elisa and Weston, an enemies-to-lovers romcom.

———

Elisa

His name is Weston Grump. I kid you not, the man's last name is Grump. It's funny, he does look like a grump. His jaw is always tight and he does seem rather serious when I've run into him in the hallway.

He's the new tenant in our building.

And from what I hear, a bachelor.

There's no ring on his finger, and I've smiled, made polite conversation a handful of times.

And he asked me out for drinks at a bar down the street. To say I'm ecstatic would be an understatement. But I know it's dangerous.

If it doesn't work out, we live in the same building.

Yikes.

He's gorgeous and easy on the eyes, with his thick, dark hair and scruffy beard. Every time I see him, he's always in a suit. He could be a professional male model. But I honestly don't know what he does for a living.

I head to the bar, having agreed to meet him there after work. I'm a little surprised he didn't offer to pick me up, since we're next-door neighbors, but I can't fault the man. Maybe he had plans before our date?

As long as it wasn't another date with someone else first.

But I'm sure he's not like that. Just because he's hot, doesn't mean he hooks up with a random girl every night.

I stalk into the bar, but he's not there. I glance at my watch. I'm two minutes early, not a lot of extra time, but I was running late curling my hair and fixing my makeup.

I grab a seat at the bar, putting my coat on the stool beside me to save Weston a seat. I order a martini and hand over my credit card to open a tab.

Wes hurries into the bar, glancing around. When he locates me, he nods and steps toward the bar counter.

I move my jacket, giving him a place to sit. He gestures to the bartender and orders a rum and Coke. "It's nice to see you again, Elisa." His gaze moves over my dress. "You look very nice."

"Thank you, you don't look so bad yourself," I say with a smirk.

He grabs his glass and takes a swig, offering me a nod. "How long have you lived in our building?"

The way he calls it *our* building sends a warm jolt of lightning through me. I tuck a strand of hair behind my ear. "Three years," I say. "Almost four. What about you? You moved from Denver, is that right?"

He cocks a sly grin. "That is correct, although I don't remember telling you that."

I press my lips together and reach for my martini. The girls in the building talk, especially when it's about a handsome new guy who moved in and he's evidently single. "Word travels fast," I say, and sip my drink. Guilty as charged.

"Gossiping will get you nowhere in life," Weston says. The smile fades from his face as he glances at my drink and then at me. "Have you eaten dinner?"

I shake my head. "I just got off work. Looking forward to a nice long weekend before I have to face my new boss."

He nods but doesn't say anything. Weston takes another swig of his rum and Coke. "We should get some food." He stalks across the bar for an empty booth and waits for me to get up to join him.

"Okay," I say, and climb down from the barstool. I grab my coat and purse, taking everything with me to the booth.

Weston examines the menu while I return back to the bar counter to grab my drink. The waitress is already at the table, taking his order.

"We'd like an order of Philly cheesesteak meatballs, mozzarella sticks, quesadillas, nachos, one pound pretzel, and artichoke and quinoa stuffed mushrooms." The waitress scribbles it all down before rushing off to put the order into the computer.

"That's a lot of food for one person," I say, sliding into the booth and placing my drink on the table. I reach for the menu to look it over.

"I ordered for both of us."

"I can't have dairy," I say. Most of what he ordered would make me sick. Six months ago, I had emergency surgery, and my gallbladder was removed. Since then, I've been plagued with lactose intolerance.

"Then I guess you can have the pretzel."

"Or I can find something on the menu to eat," I say, and open the menu, finding something that looks appetizing. I gesture the waitress over and add an order of wings.

"Anything else?" she asks.

"That's it for me."

Weston stares at his phone, nestled in his hand. He seems more interested in his smartphone than me at the moment. "I'll have a Flaming Dr. Pepper. Do you want another drink?" He doesn't so much as glance up at the waitress.

"I'll have another martini. Thank you," I say as she hurries off to put the rest of our order into the system.

"Everything okay?" I ask.

"Yeah, it's nothing." He shoves his phone into his pocket.

"Work?" I guess.

"Just family stuff." He doesn't elaborate. "You've been in the building three years, you mentioned. I take it you like it?"

"It's nice. I haven't had any issues with any other tenants."

"Good." His eyes wander toward the bar, and I shift uncomfortably as he stares at a blonde with another guy. They're having drinks in the spot we vacated.

"Do you know her?" I ask.

"Who?" Weston gives me the clueless look, but I get the feeling that she might be an ex.

It doesn't matter. "No one." I exhale a sigh and finish the last of my martini, relieved when the waitress brings a second one to the table, just in time.

———

There have been rumors that our boss, the Executive Producer and, more importantly, head of acquisitions was leaving. I'm not sure whether it was willingly or not, but the gossip has been spreading like wildfire.

"Elisa, oh my gosh, you got your hair cut short and I love the new color. It's cute!" Sloane is chipper this morning.

"It looks okay?" I ask, worried that it didn't turn out after the disaster of a date.

"Of course. Why?"

I exhale a breathy laugh. "Well, my next-door neighbor, and hot date, set my hair on fire."

"What? No way!"

I wish I were joking. "Well, it wasn't his fault. The waitress got bumped into when she lit the flame and the next thing I know, my head is slammed against the table and there's a jacket on my face. Utterly romantic and mortifying," I mutter.

"Did you get burned?" Sloane asks, her eyes wide. She glances me over, but she doesn't see any evidence of the fire. That's because there isn't any, except for my hair, which went up in seconds.

"No, thankfully, my date was quick to act and pretty much beat me with his coat."

"Sounds sexy. I'm glad you're okay."

"Thanks, and it really wasn't. It was embarrassing and just awful. I mean, the date went from bad to worse."

"Wait?" Sloane's mouth drops. "That wasn't the worst part?"

"No, it probably was, but he kept eyeing this blonde girl, like he wanted to be with her instead of me." I tug my bottom lip between my teeth. "Bad date."

"Date from hell," Sloane corrects me. "Oh, did you hear that we're getting a new head of acquisitions? Rumor has it that some new bigwig from out west is getting the Executive Producer role and we'll be forced to report to him."

"I saw John clean out his desk on Friday. Have you seen who they hired?" I keep hoping they'll promote someone on our team.

"I caught a glimpse of him when he met with HR this morning, and let me tell you, girl, he's eye candy." Sloane's cheeks are red as she fans her face.

"Yeah? When do we meet him?" Not that I'm excited to gain a new boss, but reporting to the CEO has been difficult, since he's never at the office. He works at a different location, and our Executive Producer typically had direct contact with the CEO.

"You get to meet him now," a deep voice says, and I inhale sharply. "Weston Grump, and don't you dare comment on my last name."

My tongue swipes across my top lip. How long had he been standing out in the hallway? How much had he heard?

"Mr. Grump," I say, and stand, holding out my hand to properly introduce myself. "Elisa Emerson, I'm your acquisitions editor."

"Wonderful," he says, staring at me, locking eyes, and the air seems to be sucked out of the room.

"I'm Sloane Michaels," my colleague says, standing up to introduce herself.

"Nice to meet you, Ms. Michaels," Weston says.

"Just call me Sloane. We're all pretty informal around here."

I'm glad Sloane is talking, because, right now, my mouth is prickly like a cactus. Does Weston recognize me? The last time he saw me on Friday night, my hair was long, blonde, and lit on fire.

After that disaster, I bolted and went home, vowing never to see him again.

On Saturday, I made an emergency appointment at the hairdresser's. I had her fix the disaster, and in the process of cutting, we also did a full color. With my pale skin, I look a bit gothic for my taste, but I don't care. I'm grateful for the change.

Is it possible Weston doesn't know I'm the girl from Friday night? He hasn't let on, other than the long stare. Maybe he thinks I'm familiar? I'll go with that. But it's not like a name like Elisa is all too common.

"Miss Emerson, I suggest you grab a paper and pen. My office. Ten minutes." He turns and heads back toward his private office.

"What do you think he wants?" Sloane asks, wiggling her eyebrows suggestively.

"Stop it," I hiss, glaring at her. I don't have the courage to tell her that *he* was my lousy date. "He's our boss."

"And he's hot as sin. Girl, let me have the fantasy, at least until he starts bossing us all around."

"You know he will," I say. "With a surname like Grump, it's inevitable." I don't tell her how he was an awful date. And while catching my hair on fire wasn't his fault, him constantly ogling the blonde and checking his phone was entirely on him.

I guess he had a thing for blondes. It's a good thing I'm no longer his type.

Sloane's laughter bounces off the open walls. "Girl, get it together." My eyes widen, and I dread that Mr. Grump might come out to see what all the fuss is about. There's no chance we're letting him in on the joke.

Although it kind of feels like the joke is on me, having gone out with him.

Chalk it up to experience and lousy dating apps. You have to kiss a lot of frogs to meet your prince. And Weston Grump is one hundred percent a frog. I mean, he's easy on the eyes, has a gorgeous body, and that smile, when he offers it, makes my heart strum, and I get those tingly flutters that make me flush. But he's still a grump.

I grab a pen from my desk and a blank notepad to jot down whatever Mr. Grump wants to discuss. I head for his office and give a firm knock before entering.

"Come in," he says, and I step into his office. "Shut the door behind you."

I inhale a nervous breath and try not to let him see my hand tremble. "You wanted to see me, Mr. Grump."

"Call me Weston." He glances up from his desk, not amused. "Take a seat." He gestures to the empty chair across from his desk.

"Yes, sir." I follow his instructions. It's not that big of a deal, him having me sit in his office. I'm sure that I'll have to work with him quite a bit if I'm going to be working under him. Unless he realizes that he hates it here, and there's a chance he'll move on, go and work someplace else?

"How long have you been with the company, Miss Emerson?" he asks, respecting my request to be addressed by my last name.

"Seven years, sir."

"And in that time, have you ever met the CEO?"

I inhale sharply. "No." My brow tightens. What is this line of questioning about?

"Pen. Paper?"

"Right here," I say, tapping my uncapped pen against the blank slate. "Do you have a meeting, sir? You mentioned that I would need to take notes."

"That was an assumption that you made, taking notes. I need you to draft a proposal that will be going out company-wide and then to our PR department."

"Okay," I say, unsure what I'll be writing.

"The CEO of Blazing Media, my father, passed away last night. I have taken over the company as per the terms of his last will and testament—" Weston stares at me. "Why aren't you writing?"

"Oh, right. Sorry, Mr. Grump." I jot down the information that Weston provides me with, which isn't very much.

"With the passing of my father and his absence from the media house, I am the new CEO." His eyes narrow. "Scratch that. Put something like, in this unforeseen circumstance, Mr. Weston Grump has been appointed the new CEO. While there will be changes in the coming future, everyone can rest assured that Blazing Media will continue to produce romance films for the foreseeable future."

I jot down as much as I can, but my wrist cramps, and Mr. Grump doesn't seem to notice.

"I'm sorry for the loss of your father," I say.

"Save it, Miss Emerson. Your sucking up won't do you a lick of good around here." There's a harshness that resonates with him, but I want to believe it's because he's grieving, and his father just passed away unexpectedly. "I need a draft of that typed out and on my desk within the hour."

It's not a question. "Of course, I will get right on that," I say.

He stares at me. "You're dismissed."

My jaw drops. "I have a question for you, Mr. Grump."

His nostrils flare. "I hope you take direction better when you write, because your listening skills are significantly lacking. It's Weston. Call me Weston." His jaw is clenched as he glares at me. When he realizes that I'm not leaving his office, he gestures to speak. "Go on."

"Will you be hiring a replacement for the Executive Producer position? Sloane and I thought that you were the new hire this morning," I say, putting the cap back on my pen.

"No, we will be under a hiring freeze for the next several months while I examine the books and our profitability to see what is and isn't working around here. My father, technically stepfather, wasn't very hands-on with the company. I intend to change that moving forward."

Mr. Grump stands and heads to the office door, opening it.

"You will be reporting directly to me, Miss Emerson. I expect that letter on my desk in fifty-five minutes."

"Yes, sir."

I hurry out of his office and back to my desk. In a matter of minutes, I'm tapping away at the keyboard.

"So, any gossip?" Sloane asks.

"He wants me to draft a company-wide memo," I say.

"Anything juicy?"

"I'll give you one hint; he's not the Executive Producer."

Her eyes widen. "Savage. Who is he? What's his role?"

I click away at the keys on the computer, trying my damnedest to get the memo finished ahead of schedule. Not like Mr. Grump gave me a lot of time to finish the email.

"You'll have to wait," I say, not ready to spill his secrets. She'll find out when he sends the companywide email to all employees.

Sloane stares at his office like she's envisioning the man naked or something. I swear she's drooling and obsessed with him. "He's hot. Any word on if he's married?"

That would be my luck. The bachelor in apartment 4B isn't actually a bachelor. Wouldn't be the first time that I was duped. But I haven't seen any signs of a wife or girlfriend. No ring for starters, and his office is pretty bare of any pictures. But it's only his first day.

"I don't think he is, but he's off-limits. Trust me," I say without elaborating.

"Obviously, Elisa. He's our boss. But I swear he could be an underwear model."

"Trust me. He's not worth it. The good-looking ones all think they're hot shit. Mr. Grump may be dreamy, but I'm sure that in bed his dick is a little pecker, and he can't even rock the boat. He probably keeps a cucumber in there, so girls think he's got a giant dick, but in reality, it's like one of those mini cucumbers."

A thick, heavy voice clears his throat. "Elisa, my office now!" he snaps at me.

Sloane bursts out laughing, and I throw my pen at her. She dodges the missile, grinning at me like she's proud that I got called to the principal's office.

Fuck.

Am I about to get fired?

I bring my laptop with me, grabbing it from the dock. If Mr. Grump requires that I take more notes, it'll be easier doing so with the laptop.

He lets me step into his office first, and then he slams the door abruptly behind himself.

I inhale sharply, and there's a chill in the air. My arms are covered in goosebumps.

"Do you find it appropriate to talk about my junk to another staff member?"

"I don't know what you're talking about," I say, trying to think up any excuse to escape this new brand of hell I've found myself involved in.

But there's no way out. I did this to myself and I'm going to have to pay for it.

One-click Bachelor Grump now!

ABOUT THE AUTHOR

Willow Fox has loved writing since she was in high school (many ages ago). Her small town romances are reflective of living in a small town in rural America.

Whether she's writing romance or sitting outside by the bonfire reading a good book, Willow loves the magic of the written word.

She dreams of being swept off her feet and hopes to do that to her readers!

Visit her website at:

https://authorwillowfox.com

ALSO BY WILLOW FOX

Dangerous Boss

Bossy Single Dad Series

Billionaire Grump

Mountain Grump

Bachelor Grump

Faking it with the Billionaire

Looking for kinkier books? Try these spicy stories written under the name Allison West.

Boxsets

Academy of Littles

Western Daddies Collection

Obey Daddy Collection

The Alpha Collection

Western Daddies

Her Billionaire Daddy

Her Cowboy Daddy

Her Outlaw Daddy

Her Forbidden Daddy

Standalone Romances

The Victorian Shift

Jailed Little Jade

Prefer a sweeter romance with action and adventure?
Check out these titles under the name Ruth Silver.

Aberrant Series

Love Forbidden

Secrets Forbidden

Magic Forbidden

Escape Forbidden

Refuge Forbidden

Boxsets

Gem Apocalypse

Nightblood

Royal Reaper

Royal Deception

Standalones

Stolen Art